SAVING OWEN'S TOAD

Juanita Havill

Hyperion Books for Children
New York

To Andrea Cascardi

FIRST EDITION
1   3   5   7   9   10   8   6   4   2

Havill, Juanita.
Saving Owen's Toad/Juanita Havill—1st ed.
p.   cm.
Summary: The fighting between nine-year-old Owen
and his older brother, Richard, increases when they both become interested
in toads, but for very different reasons.
ISBN 0-7868-0029-1 (trade)—ISBN 0-7868-2024-1 (lib. bdg.)
[1. Brothers—Fiction.   2. Toads—Fiction.]
I. Title.   PZ7.H31115Sav   1994   [Fic]—dc20
94-8794   CIP   AC

CONTENTS

1	*Bufo americanus*	1
2	The Cemetery	9
3	Richard's Plan	15
4	Buffy	25
5	Toad Prison	33
6	Mom Steps In	43
7	The Pond at Night	48
8	Sneak!	57
9	A Safe Place	68
10	Rescue Attempt	77
11	The Secret	87
12	Through a Toad's Eyes	95
13	No Toads Allowed	98
14	Like a Target	108
15	Saving Buffy	117

1
BUFO AMERICANUS

"Owen! Hey, Owen! Come on."

From where Owen sat, leaning against the railing of the open porch, he could hear his brother Richard yelling. Owen didn't answer. If his big brother wanted him, he would have to come upstairs to the porch and get him. Richard wouldn't come. Not right away. He would march around downstairs for a while, yelling and getting mad. Then Owen would have a little more time to read.

He looked back at his book. It was about toads. A toad's life begins as a tiny black speck in a string of clear jelly. There are thousands of specks. They are toad eggs, all laid by one mother toad and fertilized by a father toad. Toad parents don't stick around. They are long gone by the time the tiny black tadpoles hatch and squirm out.

Too bad, Owen thought. Just when they need someone to look out for them.

Owen heard footsteps in the hall.

"So there you are. Didn't you hear me?" Richard pounded on the porch door. It was locked. Owen always took the key from the door and locked it from the porch side.

Owen closed his book in slow motion. Then he got up and unlocked the door.

"I've been screaming my lungs out," Richard said. "Look, Mom wants you to run over to tell Grandma we're leaving soon. You're supposed to wait there. We'll pick both of you up after we get gas in the car."

Owen shoved his book into his khaki knapsack and stepped into the hall. He closed and locked the door, leaving the key in it. "Then are we going to the cemetery?"

"Yeah. I get to start the car. Mom will probably let me back out, too."

"I bet she won't," Owen said. Anyway, Dad wouldn't. He said Richard couldn't even practice driving until he was in high school. "You're not old enough."

"Look who's talking. The baby of the family. It'll be ages before you can drive."

"Seven years," Owen said. He had heard Richard say that you could get a license when you're sixteen.

"If you pass the test," Richard said, as if he knew Owen could never do that.

Owen was sure that if Dad were here instead of working in Ohio for two months, Richard wouldn't get to do half the things he talked Mom into letting him do. With Dad gone, Richard acted like the big boss. He bossed Elke around, too, but not as much as Owen. Elke was eleven, only two years younger than Richard. She stood up to him sometimes. It was easier for her.

Owen shouldered his knapsack and skittered past Richard. "Try not to wreck the car," he said, dodging Richard's fists and running down the hall to the stairs.

Outside, Owen shifted his knapsack to his back and marched to the alley. He tramped along the gravel, then turned to cut through the backyard past the kitchen garden Grandma had planted behind her house. It wasn't her house really. She rented the second floor from Mr. Weaver, who worked at night and slept all day.

Grandma stood on the porch, looking up at the overcast sky. When Owen saw her turn around and smile at him, he stood taller and took longer steps. He almost stumbled when something moved near him in the grass.

"A frog! Grandma, did you see that frog?" Owen dropped to his knees in the tangle of tiger lily leaves.

Drops of dew splattered his hands, and he could feel the dampness of the ground through his trousers.

"Maybe I can catch him."

"Oh dear, I'm afraid I didn't see him, Owen. And I don't want to see the look on your mother's face when she lays eyes on your Sunday trousers."

Owen backed off from the tiger lily jungle and stood up. He brushed the thick brown stain on his right knee.

"I forgot," he said. "I just wanted to see that frog up close. I could have caught him."

"I believe you could," said Grandma. "Now what brings you here? I was just getting ready to walk on over to your place."

"Mom's coming to get us—with Elke and Richard—as soon as she gets gas in the car."

Grandma bunched a bouquet of fresh-picked flowers under her left arm and held out her right hand to Owen. "Let's see if we can do something about those trousers. Your mother will want you to look nice. The preacher's going to do a Memorial Day talk at the cemetery. Lots of people will be there. Aunt Margaret and Uncle Homer and your cousins are coming over for lunch afterward."

Owen went inside with Grandma. They climbed the steep steps to the second floor and went down the hall to the bathroom. Owen set his knapsack down and climbed up on the chest by the sink.

"Aren't daffodils grand?" Grandma laid the bright yellow flowers in the bathtub. "Giant daffodils always make me think of Sinclair. Your grandfather was just crazy about them. He loved flowers. Flowers and creatures."

Grandma rinsed her hands and worked at the mud stain with a rough, soapy washcloth.

"What do you mean 'creatures,' Grandma?"

Grandma looked at Owen. "You know. Frogs and toads and snakes. He liked bugs, too, if you can imagine. He was forever studying the creeping, crawling, hopping things."

"I like creatures, too, Grandma. Nobody else does at my house. But I like frogs and toads and snakes and some bugs. I don't like mosquitoes, though."

"Nobody likes mosquitoes."

"Toads do," Owen joked. "They eat them."

Grandma laughed. Her eyes squinted almost shut, and she shook her head. "You sound like your grandpa. You even look like him, too, with your straight sandy hair and your gray eyes. It's a pity you didn't get to know each other. You would have been a pair for sure."

The crinkles around Grandma's eyes looked wet. "There," she said. "Most of the mud's off that knee. Come and I'll show you something I came across."

Owen followed Grandma into her living room

crowded with furniture. She turned the key in the glass door of her bookcase and took out the family Bible. Then she sat down in a plump faded green armchair and opened the book on her lap. Owen leaned against the chair and watched Grandma pull a loose page from the book.

"I found this last night when I was going through some old papers. I was thinking about Sinclair and suddenly, well, look what popped in front of my eyes. Maybe I should say 'hopped.' "

Owen expected to see a photo of Grandpa, a picture of him when he was a baby or a skinny boy with big eyes and shaggy blond hair, just like Owen. Grandma had said they looked alike. He was surprised to see a picture of a full-grown toad beside a clump of purple violets in the center of the page.

"Sinclair was good at drawing and painting creatures."

"Grandpa did this?" It was the best toad picture Owen had ever seen.

He couldn't read the words in spidery black cursive at the bottom of the page. "What does it say?"

"It's Latin," Grandma said. "I think it's *Bu-fo a-me-ri-ca-nus.*"

"*Bufo americanus,*" Owen repeated. He closed his eyes and said the name three times as if he were reciting a spell. He always did that when he wanted to remember something. He opened his eyes and studied the picture. The fat toad was outlined in black. The toad had bumpy greenish brown skin and dark spots on its back—spots the shape and color of the mud stain that Grandma had just washed off his trousers. Owen could feel the dark yellow eye with its black slit looking at him. He touched the eye just to see if the toad would close it.

"It looks so real, Grandma."

"It ought to. Sinclair had a lot of practice. For years and years he spent all his free time tramping around looking for creatures. Then he drew them."

"Do you have more pictures?"

"I don't think so," Grandma said. "I should have kept them, but when Sinclair died and I moved here, I just didn't have enough room for everything. I gave a lot of his books and papers to the library."

"You should put this one on the refrigerator," Owen said.

"Well, maybe I should have it framed."

"Yo! Anybody there? Time to go. Owen, hurry up!" Richard's voice boomed through the screen door downstairs.

"It'll be a miracle if he doesn't wake Mr. Weaver," Grandma said.

Owen ran to the top of the stairs. "Shut up, Richard!" he shouted. "You're going to wake up—" He stopped when he saw Mr. Weaver open the door at the bottom of the stairs.

"Sorry, Mr. Weaver."

Without answering, Mr. Weaver closed the door. Owen got his knapsack and tiptoed down the stairs. Grandma followed.

Grandma sat in the front seat. Owen scooted onto the backseat beside Richard.

"You shouldn't wake up Mr. Weaver," Richard teased.

Owen tried to elbow Richard in the ribs, but Richard blocked the blows.

"Quit fighting, you two," Elke complained.

Owen settled back in the seat. He stared straight ahead and tried to ignore Richard, who chuckled softly all the way to the cemetery.

2
THE CEMETERY

Cypress Hill Cemetery spread out across two hills with a deep gully in between. Mom drove along the crunching cinder road that led to the Snyder family plot.

"Hey! There's the soldiers," Richard shouted. "Hurry, Mom. They're going to fire a salute."

As soon as the car stopped, Richard opened the back door and jumped out. Owen put his fingers in his ears and closed his eyes. He waited a moment, then opened his eyes.

"I didn't hear the guns. Don't they work?" Owen let his hands drop from his ears.

"They haven't fired yet," Elke said. "Let's go." She got out and ran after Richard. Owen wasn't sure how he felt about hearing the rifles. Once when Dad had taken Richard target shooting, he had let Owen come to watch. Every time a rifle went off, Owen had jumped—no matter if he was staring right at the rifles before they were fired. Dad never took him again.

But Owen did want to see the soldiers. He left his knapsack in the car and followed Elke to the crowd of people on the slope above the soldiers. A line of men in uniform stood at attention. They looked like statues. Nothing moved but the red-white-and-blue flag trembling in the breeze.

"Elke," Owen said. "They're not soldiers. There's Mr. Canedy." He recognized the butcher from the supermarket. Soldiers weren't supposed to be as short and round as Mr. Canedy. Soldiers were supposed to be tall and lean like the soldiers in Owen's comic books.

"Shh," Richard hissed. He stood as straight as the soldiers.

Elke whispered to Owen. "Maybe Mr. Canedy used to be a soldier before he was a butcher."

"Oh," said Owen.

"Ready," came the command from the soldier holding a sword. "Aim. Fire."

Owen had been staring at Mr. Canedy and forgot to plug his ears. The crackling explosion of the rifles made him flinch. He felt a sudden emptiness in his stomach. Then he felt light. The soldiers fired again and again. Owen clapped his hands over his ears, but he couldn't shut out the noise. He wondered if they were using real bullets. If they were, how far could the bullets go?

The blasts stopped, and Owen's voice filled the silence. "Richard, what if they hit someone?"

"They're not aiming at anyone. They're shooting over there." Richard pointed toward the line of trees below the cemetery.

Owen looked at the trees. What if someone lived beyond those trees? His heart thumped against his ribs, and he felt giddy.

Elke nudged him on the shoulder. "They shoot blanks."

"Blanks?"

"Blanks, Owen, are empty shells," Richard spoke in his expert, know-it-all voice. "They're primed so they make a noise. There's no lead, so nothing comes out. Don't you know anything?"

"If you know so much, Richard, why didn't you say so in the first place?" Owen didn't expect an answer. He just wanted to point out that Richard didn't know everything.

Mom waved at them to come. "Preacher's going to talk now," she said. "Hurry up."

Reverend Fox approached the crowd. Aunt Margaret and Uncle Homer were walking beside him. Right behind them were their four kids: Matthew, Mark, Lucy, and Joanne, who were smiling at the preacher's back as if they knew they were going to heaven.

Reverend Fox stepped in front of the crowd. "Let us pray." He raised his arms, and his black robe fluttered like crow wings in the rising breeze. "O God," he said, and a few drops of rain began to fall.

The rain was gentle and misty. No one ran for cover. Instead, the people fidgeted and listened to Reverend Fox talk about sacrifice and love and death and freedom and how grateful we all are.

Owen was grateful that Reverend Fox didn't talk for hours the way he did on Sunday mornings and that he didn't make them wait for someone to come forward and be saved. That could take a long time.

Reverend Fox invited everyone to sing "Onward, Christian Soldiers." His voice boomed out as loud as a cannon over the crowd.

"Wouldn't you know it'd rain?" Mom complained. She asked Grandma, "Would you rather sit in the car while I put the flowers on the graves?"

"A fine warm rain like this never hurt anybody," Grandma said.

They walked back to the family plot together and set out baskets and bouquets of fresh flowers. Flower-store pink roses, mums, gladiolas, and pots of red and pink geraniums decorated the gravesite. Grandma set her daffodils in a glass jar that Richard got to fill with water from the hand pump by the road.

"It looks like a party," Lucy said.

"I wish Grandpa and all his brothers and his mom and dad could get up and see it," Owen said.

"You're weird, Owen." Lucy looked down her long nose at him. "They're all dead and buried in the ground."

Owen made a face at Lucy. Sometimes older cousins could be just as bad as older brothers.

Just then Owen felt a hand on his shoulder. He turned as Richard pulled him away from the family plot.

"Look what I found," Richard said. He opened his hand, and a toad jumped onto the grass.

"This cemetery is full of toads. The place is hopping with them." Richard fell to his knees and clapped his hand over the toad.

"Let me see," said Owen.

Richard opened his hand slightly. Owen could see the toad's bulging golden eyes with black slits across them. He touched its sandpaper-rough nose. "He's beautiful."

"You'll get warts," Joanne teased. "Warts all over your hands, Richard."

Richard thrust the toad at Joanne. She shrieked and ran from him.

"You'll get warts," she shouted over her shoulder.

Owen watched as Richard calmly put the toad in his shirt pocket and buttoned it shut.

"I didn't know you liked toads," Owen said. If Richard was so crazy about toads, why hadn't he ever paid attention to Owen when he talked about toads and frogs and snakes?

"Toads are very interesting," Richard said. "I'm coming back Wednesday, when school is out."

"When?" asked Owen. "Can I come, too?"

"Yeah, maybe. I have to think this through."

Think what through? Owen wondered. Then he saw a clump of grass shake, and a toad jumped into the air and down the slope toward the gully. He thought about Grandpa, and it made him feel good to think that there were toads all over the cemetery where Grandpa was buried.

3
RICHARD'S PLAN

"Just look at that, would you." Richard shook his head at the buckets of rain plopping onto the patio.

Owen looked up from the counter where he sat eating breakfast. He watched Richard turn from the screen door and punch his right fist into his left hand.

"No more baseball practice. And the game'll be called off."

"It always rains when summer vacation starts," Owen mumbled through a mouthful of muffin. He didn't like the rain, either. He wanted to play outside, but he didn't see why Richard had to have a fit. You'd think he owned the weather.

"It doesn't always rain," Richard shot back. "Darn! Fred and I have things to do."

Richard always had things to do with his best friend, Fred, Owen thought. "What things?" he asked.

"If the rain ever stops, maybe you'll see." Owen

knew Richard wasn't going to tell him now. He wouldn't even give him a hint.

Later in the morning Richard snapped at Elke because she wouldn't let him watch drag races on TV.

"Mom says we can only watch Channel 9 when she's at work," Elke told him.

Owen could feel an argument about to begin. He wasn't interested in watching drag races or PBS. He went upstairs to the open porch. If the wind didn't blow hard, he could sit on the porch and read without getting himself or his book wet. The square-shaped porch fit in the corner between the walls of the house. Beneath the porch floor was the kitchen, and above it the roof of the house jutted out. Owen had to sit against the house to keep dry. He couldn't dangle his feet between the railing slats that fenced in the other two sides the way he did when it wasn't raining.

Owen liked to come to the porch to be alone, to think, or to read. There he sat, higher up than anyone in the neighborhood. He could see for several blocks, across the treetops, the patchwork of roofs, fuzzy backyard weeds, laundry hanging in neat strips on sunny days, and battered garbage cans in pairs along the alley. He liked being up there and looking down, seeing and not being seen. Most people never even looked up.

It rained for six days. Owen read on the porch

every day. He had finished his toad book and was going to start reading it again. Then the sun came out. With sunny weather Richard quit moping and jumped into action. At least Richard ordered everybody else into action.

"Hey, Owen, go get Patrick. Tell him we're meeting in the backyard. Fred's coming in a few minutes. Elke, you call the cousins and tell them to get over here quick. I already talked to Matthew and Mark about it. They'll be ready."

"I don't want to go to Patrick's right now," Owen said. Patrick lived in the neighborhood, at the end of the alley. He was eleven, younger than Richard and Fred, but Richard usually let him hang around with them, especially when there was work to do.

"If you want to be included, then you'd better get Patrick. There's no room in my plan for people who don't cooperate."

Owen shrugged. He did want to find out what was going on. Who wouldn't? After being shut inside with Richard for six days, listening to him grumble about not being able to do "important things," Owen was curious to find out just what these important things were.

Owen went out the back door and started up the alley. He was glad to see Patrick riding on his bike toward him.

"Fred told me there's a meeting," Patrick said as he pedaled past Owen.

Figures, Owen thought. The only reason Richard told him to get Patrick was to order him around. Owen trudged back home to join Fred, Elke, Patrick, Matthew, and Mark. They all sat on the grass in front of the clubhouse. Richard stood on the club-house steps.

"How would you like to go hunting?" he asked.

"Yeah!" Matthew and Mark shouted.

"Hunting?" Owen asked uneasily. What was Richard getting at? He always went hunting with Dad. He was probably trying to make his plan sound great. He always did that to you. Then when you said, "Yes, I'll do it," you found out it wasn't so great after all.

"We couldn't go until now because of the rain," Richard said. "Listen. I'm talking about a special kind of hunting. My plan is—"

"Wait!" Owen interrupted. "Aren't Lucy and Joanne coming? We should wait, or they'll be mad."

"Lucy hates toads," Matthew said, "and so does Joanne. Shut up and let Richard tell us the plan."

"It sounds like you already know what it is," Owen said, wondering what toads had to do with it. Why would Richard want to hunt toads? Was he going to kill them? Owen was beginning not to like Richard's big plan.

"We're starting a business." Richard's brown eyes

danced as he lifted his navy blue baseball cap up, then pulled it down tightly over his buzzed black hair.

Fred stood beside him, rubbing his hands together. Fred was six months older than Richard and bigger, too, but he always let Richard do the talking.

Seeing Richard fired up about a new project made Owen feel uneasy. Sometimes Richard had funny ideas. Once Owen had gotten into big trouble for writing "The FBI is watching you" with Mom's lipstick on Mr. Weaver's window. Richard had set up a counterspy ring to keep an eye on Mr. Weaver, who, according to Richard, had suspicious habits, such as working all night. Also, Richard had seen him sending out top secret information on a radio. Mr. Weaver had caught Owen with the lipstick and had really chewed him out for not knowing the difference between a spy and an assembly-line foreman with a CB radio.

Richard hadn't gotten caught, but he had been mad at Owen for weeks. "Good spies don't reveal anything. They take poison pills," he had told Owen.

"No one has ever had a business like this," Richard said now.

"It's ingenious!" Fred raved.

Then Richard lowered his voice and said very seriously, "If we want it to work, we all have to work together."

Last fall, Owen remembered, Richard had said

the very same thing. He had talked Dad into driving them to Mr. Simpson's farm to glean the corn that the combine had missed. Then Owen, Elke, and the cousins had shucked it and popped off the dried kernels. They had worked practically all day and had made only $8.65, which, split seven ways, wasn't even enough to pay for a movie ticket. Owen had sore thumbs for weeks. Richard didn't have sore thumbs. He had been supervisor.

"I know you can't wait to hear the details." Richard paused for suspense. "We're going to start a toad farm. And sell the toads to the neighbors. Toads eat flies and mosquitoes and grungy bugs that bother people and their gardens. What every neighbor needs is a bunch of toads in the backyard. But according to research I've been doing, there is going to be a toad shortage. For no reason at all the toads are dying out in Central America—"

"Hey!" Owen shouted. "I want my *Ranger Rick* back!" He hadn't been able to find his magazine for a week.

"Relax, Owen. I'll give it back when I've finished my research."

"Do toads eat fleas?" Patrick asked. "Mom says we've got fleas from the dog, and she's going to move out if Dad doesn't sell Maggie or call the pest control person."

"Toads eat all bugs," Richard said.

How can he be so sure? Owen wondered. There might be some bugs that toads don't eat. Since when did Richard know everything there was to know about toads?

"They especially like fleas," Richard said. "Toads are great for pest control. That's what our business is all about: pest control."

"But we don't have any toads," Owen said.

Richard gave Owen a dirty look. "Sure we do." He and Fred held up two ice-cream buckets with holes poked in the plastic covers.

"Let me see," said Owen.

"No." Richard held his bucket higher. "They'll get out. And that's what we don't want. Me and Fred caught every toad in the neighborhood this morning. There were only twenty-three. If they're dying out, that makes them rare and more expensive. But we need more toads." Richard looked at Fred, and Fred nodded. "We figure we need about sixty if we sell them for a dollar apiece."

"A dollar!" Elke protested.

"Too much," Mark agreed.

"Okay," Richard said, waving his hands. "Fifty cents. But then we need one hundred and twenty toads."

"I don't get it," Owen said. "Why would people buy toads for fifty cents? Toads are everywhere—not like something you see at the store and buy."

"They will when they realize they don't have any."

"But Richard, you took their toads," Owen argued.

"Owen, how can you be so dense? Do you want to be in the business? Toads are everywhere. You said it yourself. So anyone can catch them."

"If they're everywhere, why will people buy them?" Owen muttered. He could tell that no one was paying attention to him.

"Because we're selling them. Besides, we need the money. Fred and I are saving up for bows and arrows. Real hunting bows. We'll give all of you some money for helping us. Now go get your ice-cream buckets. Meet me back here in ten minutes, and we'll ride to the cemetery. That's where we can catch a bunch of toads. So if you don't want to come, Owen, that's fine with me. Don't."

Owen remembered Memorial Day and Grandpa's grave and the toad. Now he knew why Richard wanted to go back. Owen wanted to go back, too.

"But I want to come," Owen insisted.

"So will you quit arguing?"

Owen nodded.

"But it's four blocks away," Patrick said. "I'll have to ask my mom."

"Okay. Hurry. But don't tell her why. Tell her we're going to play ball at the old softball field across the street from the cemetery."

"Okay." Patrick raced off.

"I've got buckets for you and Mark," Richard said to Matthew. "Elke—you and Owen can get some in the basement. Mom won't miss them. There's tons."

Owen ran into the house with Elke. Elke found the buckets in the fruit cellar. She handed one to Owen, and they ran back up the basement steps.

Mom met them at the door. "What are you two in such a hurry about?" she asked.

"We're going to the cemetery," Owen blurted out. Too late, he remembered Richard didn't want them to tell anybody.

"To play ball," Elke said quickly. She gave Owen a keep-your-mouth-shut stare.

"You're going to play ball at the cemetery? With ice-cream buckets?" Mom wasn't convinced.

"Oh no, Mom," Elke explained. "We're going to the ball diamond that's close to the cemetery." She held up the bucket and jiggled it. "It's easier to carry the mitts in these buckets."

Mom looked at Owen. She waited for his version. "Well, I'm going to the cemetery first," Owen said. "I'm going to Grandpa's grave."

Elke nudged him brusquely. "Look, Mom, we've got to hurry."

"I guess it's all right, but Owen, don't stay at the cemetery. You go on and play with the others. And could you check on the flowers at Grandpa's grave?"

"Sure, Mom."

"And be home, all of you, by noon."

"Okay." Elke pulled Owen by the elbow and hurried out the door. "Gosh, Owen, you and your mouth. Do you want to spoil everything?"

"I won't spoil anything," Owen said. He wasn't trying to mess up Richard's plan. He just wasn't sure he wanted to be part of it.

4

BUFFY

At first Owen tried to keep up with the others. Richard and Fred led the way, racing down Cherry Street on their ten-speeds.

"I hope we can play catch after we finish," Patrick shouted to Matthew. "I brought my mitt."

"Me, too," Matthew said. "But Richard will probably make us work all morning."

Mark shot ahead of Elke, but she stood to pedal and caught up in a minute. Soon she was in front of him. She turned and waved to Owen, who trailed them all. "Shake a leg, Owen!" she shouted.

Owen watched as Elke turned at Fifth Street and Mark followed her. Owen quit trying to pedal faster. He wheeled along at his own speed on his hand-me-down dirt bike. He was used to being last. The way he figured it, he would always be last. Richard would always be first. Elke would be in the middle, and if there were other kids along, they would be ahead of him, too.

Owen watched Richard and Fred turn left onto Cypress Hill Road. Matthew, Patrick, Elke, and Mark came next. Owen followed them to the cinder road, then up to the cedar tree beside the Snyder plot. By the time he dismounted and joined them, Richard had just finished giving instructions.

"Why do I have to hunt with Elke?" Mark complained.

"I'll catch more toads than you," she said. "Come on, fussbutt, let's go." Elke gripped her bucket and ran down the slope. Mark trudged after her. Matthew and Patrick set off in another direction.

Owen lifted his bucket from his bicycle handlebars.

"You go with Elke, too, Owen," Richard said. "And keep the lid on so the toads can't jump out of your bucket. Me and Fred are going to the far end of the gully. Scream if you need us."

"Okay." Owen watched them jog toward the end of the slope. Then they slid down the grassy hill and disappeared.

Owen turned and walked on the mowed grass path alongside the gravestones. He was careful not to walk across the graves. Elke had told him that it was bad luck to walk over the heads of the dead. They didn't like to be disturbed, she had said. Owen wasn't sure which way the dead were lying. He might end up walking over their heads instead of their feet. Even if he wasn't big and heavy and they probably wouldn't notice him, he didn't want to take any chances.

The family grave plot looked different than it had on Memorial Day. One basket of flowers had blown over, and the roses were scattered like twigs. The gladiolas sagged, and the water in their basket was green and it stank. Owen picked up the jar of daffodils and pulled them out. The big yellow flowers had turned brown at the edges. He laid them down and emptied the jar. He went to the pump to refill the jar and plopped the daffodils back into it.

He felt awkward setting the jar of flowers silently in front of the gravestone. He felt as if he ought to speak.

"We came to hunt toads, Grandpa. I'm supposed to catch some, too. We're going to sell them to the neighbors. Toads eat bugs." He stopped talking. That was a stupid thing to say. Grandpa would know that toads eat bugs. "Anyway, Richard says that everyone will want to buy them."

Owen stared intently at the grass over the grave. He watched a powdery white moth wiggle in the grass and waited for it to fly. It kept crawling through the grass toward him. Maybe he could reach down and catch it. He shifted forward and then, right at the toe of his black high-top, he saw a toad.

The toad struggled through the grass as awkwardly as the moth. Why doesn't he jump? Owen wondered.

The toad stopped suddenly and looked up. Owen was sure the round bulging eyes were aimed right at him. For a whole minute Owen and the toad stared at each other. There was no sound. Nothing moved. Nothing else in the whole universe existed but Owen and the toad. Owen felt that something incredible was about to happen. Maybe the toad would open his mouth and speak. Then Owen blinked. The toad didn't budge, as if waiting intently for something. What? Owen studied the toad. He was a dusty green, the color of the tips of quack grass. Blotches of muddy brown spread across his bumpy back. He looked as if he had jumped right out of Grandpa's drawing.

Owen moved his foot toward him, but the toad just sat there. Maybe he was waiting for Owen to pick him up. Owen made a bowl over the toad with his hands. He could feel the toad wriggling. He scooped his right hand under the toad and pinched his shoulders gently with his thumb and index finger. Then, raising the toad slightly, he closed his hand around him, letting him poke his head out above his thumb.

The toad wriggled a little, then settled onto Owen's palm.

"Hi, Toad." Owen touched the toad's rough,

rounded nose with the tip of his thumb. "You're beautiful." Then his hand felt wet as if he were holding a peeled peach.

"You don't have to pee all over me. I'm not going to hurt you. I thought you wanted me to pick you up."

Owen pulled the lid off the ice-cream bucket as he anchored it between his knees. He set the toad down quickly and popped the lid back on. He wiped his hands on his jeans, then lifted the lid a crack to peek in.

The toad crawled around the bottom of the bucket. Then it sprang awkwardly against the side of the bucket and slid back down. There was something peculiar about this toad. Owen saw that the left side of the toad was different. In place of a long leg folded against his side was a twiglike stump, half a matchstick.

"What happened to you?" Owen felt squishy in his stomach when he thought about the toad's missing leg. Had a lawn mower blade clipped off his leg? Or had the toad been born that way? "Poor toad. You need someone to take care of you," Owen said. "And you came to the right person." Maybe that was why the toad had sat and waited for Owen to pick him up.

"If I'm going to take care of you, I'll have to give you a name." The name had to be just right. Names are important. Owen had named animals before: Cooey, a pigeon with a broken wing they had kept until he got better; a baby dove named Mo that Grandma had raised and then let go; and all six of the neighbor Mr. Cunningham's cat's kittens: Darby, Alice, Whitebeard, Scuttle, Cuddle, and Sam. Owen could tell them apart, too. He could always tell animals apart.

As he watched the toad, Owen could feel the sun on his back. He wiped sweat from his upper lip with the back of his hand. A mosquito bit him twice on the ear, then landed on his shoulder. He swatted without looking and missed.

"Buffy," he said. "I'm going to call you Buffy." The toad was probably a male. His throat was kind of dark. But with a name like Buffy, it didn't really matter.

"I caught twenty toads."

Startled, Owen looked up to see Elke trotting up the hill toward him. She was so red in the face you couldn't see her freckles, and her red hair looked as tangled as a brier patch.

Mark, lagging behind, called out, "I caught some, too."

"Only five." Elke reached toward Owen's bucket. "How many did you get, Owen?"

Owen snapped the lid shut. "I caught a toad."

"Let me see." She pounced on the bucket, peeled the lid halfway off, and smiled. "Sure did. One little toad." She pressed the lid closed. "Richard might laugh at you, Owen, but that's okay. Don't let it bother you." She punched Owen lightly on the shoulder. "He's a nice toad."

Richard and Fred loped side by side up the cinder road, each carrying a bucket.

"Our buckets are full," Richard announced. "We've still got time to play ball. Did anybody bring a bat?"

"Hey, Matthew. Come on, Patrick. Let's go play ball," Fred shouted down the gully.

"We must have caught a hundred," Richard bragged. "We'd better keep the buckets in the shade. We don't want to cook any toads. We'll count them at home. Let's go." He slapped his hands together like a baseball coach.

"I'll share my mitt with you, Owen," Elke said.

"No. I'd better guard Buffy."

"Buffy?"

"I named my toad Buffy."

"That's a funny name for a toad." Elke ran off laughing.

Owen didn't have time to explain that the name Buffy came from *Bufo americanus* and that he had learned it from Grandma.

Owen pulled a clump of quack grass from beside the road. He put it in the bucket to make Buffy feel more at home. Then he sat against the cedar tree and stared down at Buffy.

"I don't want to play baseball with Richard. I never get to bat. I just chase the ball in the field, and when I throw it in, Richard says I should throw it harder."

Buffy sat so still Owen felt sure he was listening. He wondered if Grandpa had talked to his toads, too.

"I wish Grandpa could see you, Buffy. Did you know Grandpa loved creatures like you? That's what Grandma said. He could draw a picture of you, too, and it would look just like you." Owen wondered if Grandpa kept any of the animals as pets. "I'm going to keep you, Buffy," he said softly. It didn't matter if the whole idea of the toad hunt was to catch toads to sell.

"I won't let Richard have you, Buffy. No way. You're my toad. I found you, and I'm keeping you."

Owen picked up the bucket when he saw Elke ride up the cinder road. "Time to go," she said, and made a quick U-turn to rejoin the others.

Owen bent down to touch the grass in front of Grandpa's grave.

"Thanks, Grandpa," he whispered. "I'll take good care of Buffy. I promise."

5

TOAD PRISON

"Put your buckets under the maple tree in the back-yard," Richard ordered when they got home from the toad hunt. "We'll meet there after lunch, soon as Fred and me finish something important."

Owen didn't follow them through the open gate to the tree. He went the opposite direction across the patio to the back steps. He pulled the lattice screen away from the side of the steps just enough for Buffy's bucket to fit through. He set the bucket in a safe, dark corner under the steps. "I'll be back soon," he whispered. Then he went inside to wash up for lunch.

Mom had fixed tuna salad sandwiches and was plopping potato chips onto each plate. She looked up when Owen walked in. "How did the baseball game go?"

"Fine." Owen picked up the pitcher and poured milk into the glasses.

"Fine? That's all?" Mom said. "You did get to play, didn't you?"

"Uh, sure." Owen was glad that Elke and Richard rushed in just then so he didn't have to explain any details about a game of baseball he hadn't played.

Richard pounced on his sandwich.

"Whoa!" Mom said. "What's the rush?"

"Sorry, Mom," Richard explained. "I've got stuff to do this afternoon."

"That doesn't mean you have to gobble your food. By the way, I hope these things you have to do can be done close to home. When I'm at work, I'd like for you three to stick around. Okay?"

"No problem," Richard said as he stuffed a quarter of his sandwich into his mouth.

As soon as he finished, Richard jumped up, grabbed two ginger cookies from a plate on the table, and looked at Elke, then Owen. "Ten minutes," he said. "Be there." He hurried out of the room.

Mom shook her head. "Richard has always got something going on. I wonder what it is this time?"

Elke shrugged. Owen looked down at his plate and readjusted the lettuce on his sandwich. If Elke wasn't going to say anything, neither was he. Besides, he didn't know what the whole plan was. He wondered what was going to happen next.

By the time Owen finished eating, Mom and Elke had left the table. He rinsed his plate and put it in the dishwasher, then went outside to check on Buffy.

He pulled the latticework back and reached in to grab the bucket.

"Hey, Owen!"

Owen jumped back when he heard Fred call him. He turned and leaned against the lattice.

"We need more nails, Owen. Richard says there are some in a bag in your pantry, on the counter."

"Okay. I'll get them," Owen said, and ran inside to look for the bag for Fred. Had Fred seen him reach under the porch? He didn't think so. He wanted to get Fred away from there as fast as he could. He found the bag of nails and ran back with it.

"Here. These are super-big nails. What do you need them for?"

"You'll see." Fred hurried back to the clubhouse.

Owen made sure no one was around this time. He reached under the porch and tapped the lid of Buffy's bucket. Then he wedged his head and shoulder through the opening and peeled the lid up enough to see the toad. "Sit tight, Buffy. I'm going to see what Richard's up to." He snapped the lid back and slipped away from the steps.

In the backyard Elke and Mark were banging on the clubhouse door. "Let us in!" she shouted.

Matthew and Patrick sat on the grass by the clubhouse waiting. Owen could hear Richard shouting at Fred. He heard loud, sharp pounding, too.

The nails, of course, but what were they building?

Fred opened the door a crack and stuck his head out. "Hold your horses. We're meeting under the maple tree. Go on. Wait for us there."

Elke and Mark turned away when the door shut. Elke motioned to Matthew and Patrick. "Come on," she said. Then she saw Owen. "You, too, Owen. We might as well wait over there."

Owen started to follow Elke. Then the clubhouse door swung open, banging against the side. Richard stepped out. Fred followed, dodging the door as it slammed back. They marched past the brick patio, around the shallow cement goldfish pond, and leap-frogged over the empty birdbath. Owen trotted after them.

Richard started talking as soon as he reached the maple tree. "Bring all your buckets to me. Make a circle around the buckets so if a toad escapes, we can catch it."

Owen watched the others set their buckets in front of Richard. Fred took two buckets from behind the maple and set them with the others.

"Okay, Fred." Richard waved his hand toward the clubhouse and Fred trotted off.

"Why can't we meet in the clubhouse, too?" Patrick asked.

"It's too hot."

"You and Fred were in the clubhouse."

"Look, we're meeting out here. We had things to do. That's all."

Fred clambered out of the clubhouse holding a wide plywood slab like a tray. On it was a lopsided wooden crate.

So that's what they were pounding on, Owen thought. An orange crate with a screen wrapped around it. He could see that the top screen was held shut with a green metal wire twisted through the side screen.

"This is our toad cage," Richard said. He lifted it off the plywood tray. "And this is the raft. We're going to keep the toad cage on a raft in the middle of the goldfish pond. That will keep them from escaping."

"Can't toads swim?" Mark asked.

"Yeah, but they don't like to," Richard answered. "They can't swim very fast anyway, so whoever is guarding them will have time to catch them when they reach the edge." Richard paused. "Any questions?"

Owen didn't like this idea one bit, but he could see that Richard had already made up his mind. The others didn't say anything.

"Okay, Fred, open the hatch. Come on, guys. Come up close so you can watch them. If they jump out, catch them. Let's start with my bucket."

Fred held the screen door open. Richard tore the lid from his bucket.

Owen leaned forward. Wow! Richard must have a hundred toads. Toad upon toad, crammed and cramped in that bucket. The toads on top began to hop as Richard tipped the bucket and dumped them into the cage. Richard grabbed one toad that clung to the screen and dropped it onto the others. Then Fred closed the screen door.

"Next," Richard said, wiping his hands on his jeans.

Elke picked up her bucket and handed it to Richard. He took the lid off. Fred opened the screen and down slid twenty toads. The last one needed prompting. Elke reached in to poke it, and it jumped into the cage.

"That sure is a lot of toads," Mark said.

Too many, Owen thought. They shouldn't be scrunched together. They looked miserable.

First Richard emptied Patrick's bucket, then Matthew's, then Mark's. "We should have more than this." Richard turned to Owen. "Where's your bucket, Owen? How many toads did you catch?"

"I didn't catch any," Owen said.

"None?" Richard said. "In all that time, not one?"

"But what did you do with your toad?" Elke blurted out.

Owen scowled at her. Why did she have to open her big mouth?

Fred nudged Richard, then leaned over to tell him something. Owen couldn't hear him, but when Fred took off toward the patio, Owen ran after him. By the time Owen caught up, Fred had jerked the lattice open. He grabbed the bucket with one hand, and Owen charged him. Fred shoved Owen so hard that Owen lost his balance and fell. As soon as he got up, he ran after Fred. Richard already held the bucket when Owen tried to grab it from him, but Fred blocked him and wrapped his arms around him in a bear hug.

Owen struggled as he watched Richard take off the lid.

"You only got one?" Richard said. "I guess one toad is better than none."

"I want to keep him in my bucket!" Owen shouted.

"Look, Owen, you went toad hunting with the rest of us. If you want to get paid, you have to put your toad in the cage like everyone else so we can sell him."

"I don't want to get paid. I don't want to sell Buffy."

"What's this Buffy stuff?"

"That's his name. I named him. He's my toad, and I don't want to sell him."

Richard picked Buffy up. "This toad is weird. He's only got three legs."

"Let Owen keep him." Elke spoke up. "Nobody will buy a three-legged toad, anyway."

Ignoring Elke, Richard opened the screen and dropped Buffy into the cage onto the mound of toads.

Owen twisted frantically in Fred's grip until he wriggled free. He lunged at Richard, then stopped when Richard pulled his fist back to his shoulder, ready to punch Owen. Owen gritted his teeth, but he didn't flinch or cower. He was too mad at Richard to be afraid. He grabbed the cage door, but Fred held it closed as Richard twisted the metal wire to fasten it.

"Let me have Buffy back!" Owen screamed. He stared into the toad faces and toad eyes. He couldn't even find Buffy now. He tried to cling to the wire cage as Richard peeled his fingers from it.

"Don't be a baby, Owen. Listen, I'll let you shoot my bow when I get it."

"I don't want to shoot your bow. I want Buffy."

"Okay. If we don't sell him, you can have him."

"I want him now," Owen said.

"Then you'll just have to buy him back. And since you're causing so much trouble, you'll have to pay a dollar. I was counting on you catching more than one toad, remember."

"A dollar? I don't have a dollar. I'll have to ask Mom."

"If you say anything about this to Mom, I'll sell your toad first."

"I've got some money," Elke said. "Maybe there's enough."

Owen watched Richard and Fred launch the raft into the goldfish pond. Owen's stomach lurched upward as the raft plunged into the water. The sides weren't high enough, and water splashed over the edge, leaving puddles on the raft. Toads hopped and climbed on the screen as the raft drifted two feet from the edge of the small pond. Owen could feel their fear. And he felt something else. Anger. He was so mad at Richard that he had to blink when he looked at him. He was filled up to the top with anger.

Richard tied the cord from the raft around the cement seat at the pond's edge.

"Matthew—you and Patrick are first guards. The rest of us are going around the neighborhood to take orders for toads. We'll deliver them later. Fred, come on. We'll go up Fifth Street. Elke—you and Mark take Sixth."

"I'm not going yet," Elke said. "I have to see how much money I have."

"Well, I'm not going alone," Mark fussed.

"What a bunch of duds," said Richard. "Come on, Fred, let's get out of here before Matthew and Patrick start whining, too."

"You better not sell Buffy." Owen sank down beside the pond and stared at the raft. His throat ached as he tried to keep from crying. Where was Buffy? What would happen to him?

"Come on, Owen. I'll help you find some money." Elke tugged at his elbow. "Richard will let you buy your toad back. You'll see."

Owen got to his feet, letting Elke lead him to the back door. He didn't see how Elke could trust Richard. He had stolen Buffy and put him in a toad prison. Owen couldn't believe anything Richard said.

6

MOM STEPS IN

"Twenty-five. Twenty-six. Twenty-seven. Twenty-eight." Owen counted a handful of pennies on the rug in the middle of Elke's room.

"Good," Elke mumbled, her back to Owen. She rummaged through her dresser drawers. Suddenly she jerked a quilted purse from the top drawer and thrust her hand into it. "Here's a quarter." She showed Owen. Then she dumped out a round leather coin purse from the quilted bag and pried it open. "Two cents."

Owen left his coins on the rug and went over to the window. From there he could look down at the fishpond. The raft floated right in the middle. Patrick and Matthew were arm wrestling near the pond.

"Hey, why don't you help me?" Elke said. "It's for *your* toad!"

"I don't know where to look," Owen said, without taking his eyes off the raft.

"You could start with those drawers." Elke pointed to the chest in the corner.

Owen shrugged and swallowed hard. He left the window to yank at the bottom drawer, which fell with a clunk on his right foot. "Ow." He winced and felt tears start to fill his eyes.

"Don't pull so hard, Owen."

"I didn't. It just slipped out. It's a dumb drawer."

"No, it isn't dumb. It's just a drawer."

"It's a dumb drawer, and there's no money in it, not even a little penny, and there's no way I can buy Buffy." Owen sat down beside the drawer, took off his shoe, and held his sore foot. It was another hurt to add to the one that ached inside. He was the only one who cared about Buffy, but he wasn't big enough or strong enough to make Richard give him back. He wasn't even good enough at arguing.

"Wait, Owen. I bet Mom has some pennies." Elke gathered up the change on the rug and added her coins to it. "Fifty-five cents. Look, Owen, we can get a dollar, easy."

Rubbing his foot, Owen shook his head.

"But sometimes Mom gives you change, doesn't she?"

Owen stared at Elke. She was right. Mom did give him her loose change from the bottom of her purse.

"Richard!" Mom's voice rang out from downstairs. "Richard! Ri-chard!"

"Mom's mad," Owen said.

Elke shouted down the stairs. "Richard isn't up here, Mom. He's outside somewhere."

"Then, Elke, you come down here for a minute." Mom was standing at the bottom of the stairs.

Owen followed Elke down.

"I would like to know what that old crate is doing in the fishpond."

"Richard put it there with Fred," Elke said.

"I thought so. And where is Richard now?"

"He's taking orders for toads," Elke answered.

"He's got a hundred toads in that cage," Owen said. He figured if Elke could talk about the toads to Mom, he could, too. And he would tell Mom everything. "He put Buffy in the cage, too, and now I can't buy him because I don't have enough money."

"Owen, what are you talking about? Try to calm down," Mom said. "So where did you get these toads?"

Owen and Elke looked at each other. "We caught them."

Then Elke added, "To sell."

"No, we didn't," Owen said. "Not all of us. I don't want to sell Buffy."

"Sell? What kind of an idea is that?" Mom said.

Owen wasn't sure if she expected an answer to that question or not. "A dumb idea. And I want Buffy back," he said anyway, because it was true.

"We'll have to see about that. I'm going to talk to Richard as soon as he comes home."

"Mom, can I have some pennies?" Owen asked.

"We'll see." Mom turned and walked briskly toward the kitchen.

Owen and Elke went back upstairs. Owen hovered near the window while Elke put things back in her drawers. He saw Matthew and Patrick go into the clubhouse. They came out laughing and ran out the gate into the neighbor's yard.

"They're not very good guards," Owen said. Now that they were gone, maybe he could run down and get Buffy out.

Too late. Richard and Fred walked into the yard. They talked for a minute, then Fred waved to Richard and trotted back up the alley toward home.

"Richard!" Mom shouted from the kitchen door.

Owen and Elke ran to the guest bedroom, the one beside the open porch and above the kitchen. They pressed their ears against the heat register that covered the duct from the basement. The duct ran through the kitchen, so they could hear Mom and Richard talking.

"I want those toads set free and that crate out of the pond, Richard."

"But they're all right, Mom. Besides, we've already sold ten of them."

"Sold them?"

"Yeah. To the Ragsdales and the Steins and Mrs. Hunter on the corner."

"Richard. All I can say is that you had better sell the others pretty quick."

"I will, Mom."

"In about half an hour, Richard."

"Aw, Mom. I can't do that. I've got a ball game."

"Richard."

"Tomorrow. I'll sell them all tomorrow. I promise. Fred even needs some for his mom's garden."

"All right, Richard, but there is one mom who doesn't want any toads. Okay? Now get into your baseball uniform. We'll go out for a quick supper before the game."

Elke jumped up. "We're going to eat hamburgers and french fries, and there's a baseball game tonight. I've got to get my baseball cap." She ran down the hall to her room.

Owen remained against the register, wondering how Elke could forget so quickly about Buffy and the money. He strained to hear Mom's voice. Nothing. She had finished talking. She hadn't said a word about Buffy.

7

THE POND AT NIGHT

Owen didn't play on a baseball team. He hadn't tried out in April. Why bother? He fumbled a lot and was a lousy batter. In gym class when it was his turn to bat, his whole team yelled at him, "Don't swing! Just watch the ball." That's because he was small and it would be easy for him to get walked. But Owen wanted to hit the ball so bad, he always swung at it. And he always struck out. That's probably why he was the last one picked for a team in gym. In Little League it would have been the same except he wouldn't have gotten to play at all.

But Owen didn't mind going to games. On any other night but tonight he would have wanted to go. He liked to wait for the lights perched over the diamond to blink on at dusk. He liked to hang from the bars above the top bleacher, then drop in the dust and run to the swings behind left field. He also liked to eat the Fudgsicles that Mom let him and Elke buy at the concession stand. But tonight Owen wanted to stay home. He didn't want to swing with Elke or eat Fudgsicles or watch Richard hit a home run. He wanted to stay in the backyard and keep an eye on Buffy.

Mom wouldn't let him stay. "Grandma is playing bridge tonight. There is no way I will let you stay alone while the rest of us go to the baseball game, Owen. Now hurry. We'll barely have time to eat hamburgers at Sandy's before the game."

They sat in a booth at Sandy's Quik Burger. Owen chewed his hamburger as if it were cardboard. Across from him Richard pigged down two burgers. How could Richard act as if nothing had happened? Elke didn't have trouble eating, either. She sat beside Richard, dipping each french fry into her strawberry milkshake before dribbling it into her mouth.

All Owen could think about was Buffy. Was he hungry? Was he being squashed to death?

"Hurry up, slowpoke." Richard got up. "Hey, Mom, let's go. I've got to warm up my pitching arm."

Owen glared at him as Mom and Elke gathered the cups and napkins and stood to leave. Then Owen squished his hamburger and bun into a gooey ball and crammed it back into the paper bag. He left the bag on the table and followed the others to the car.

At the ball game Owen sat with Elke on the top

bleacher. The game dragged on forever. Richard's team was way ahead. Ten to one. Mom hadn't yelled at the umpire once. Richard hadn't hit a home run, either.

"You should have seen that!" Mom called out suddenly. "Richard belted a line drive to center field and made it to third base."

Owen didn't say anything. He dropped from the bleacher bar to the dust below and made mud drawings with a stick in the puddle of Fudgsicle. He had let his melt instead of eating it.

Elke dragged him to the swings at the end of the fifth inning. He sat hunched in a swing while Elke pumped and rose into the night sky. Owen kept thinking about Buffy scrunched together with a hundred other toads in a cage, floating in the middle of the pond. It wasn't right. There was nothing for the toads to eat. They didn't have enough room, either. They were probably jumping all over each other, and maybe Buffy was on the bottom. Buffy had only three legs. He couldn't hop like the other toads. He would get mashed in that toad cage. Owen had to rescue Buffy. Tonight. When everyone was asleep, he would go out to the pond and find Buffy and take him out of the cage. Guards or no guards, he had to get Buffy out!

Finally the game ended, and they went home. Richard's team had won, of course, and it took everyone a while to calm down. Owen couldn't calm down either, but his excitement had nothing to do with the game. He thought Mom would never come upstairs to bed. He lay in his undershorts on the bottom bunk beneath Richard in the room they shared. He had already noticed that Elke was asleep in her cot in the porch room. She slept there in summer because her room on the west side of the house got too hot.

Light from Mom's room filled the hallway. She was still reading her mystery book. Owen lay back on his pillow, waiting and listening. The roaring hum of locusts drilled into his ears. How could anyone sleep through that noise? Then he thought that maybe the noise was a good thing. Maybe the locusts would make such a racket that no one would hear him when he got up.

At last Mom switched her light off. Owen listened for what seemed like a year until he heard Mom's soft snoring blend with the locust drone. He eased out of bed, took two steps backward, and stood on tiptoe to see if Richard was asleep. Like a baby, the baseball hero snoozed on his back.

Barefoot, Owen padded down the stairs. He took the shiny metal flashlight from the kitchen drawer. Then he unlocked the screen door and stepped into the hot, soggy air. A moonless night, it was so dark that he had to feel his way down the back porch steps. He didn't want to use his flashlight until he was sure no one was there. The locusts were even louder under the trees. They sounded like jackhammers breaking up a highway.

The shadowy forms of trees looked spooky, especially the giant maple above the pond. Its black leaves trembled in the hot breeze. Owen shivered despite the sticky heat. He stared until his eyes hurt. He wanted to make sure that Fred or someone else wasn't on night patrol. It would be hard for the kids to sneak out at night, but you never knew about Richard. He could have figured something out.

Owen scooped up a rock and tossed it toward the pond. It thumped on the ground, but no one appeared. "Face it," Owen told himself, "you're the only kid out here tonight." He turned on the flashlight and followed its round glow to the pond.

He beamed light onto the pond and centered the spotlight on the toad cage. He gasped. The raft was sinking. The far end had almost gone under. Water filled the bottom of the toad cage. Toads were crawling on top of one another, pulling themselves up by the screen.

Oh no! Buffy's going to be smashed for sure and drowned. Owen set the flashlight on the concrete edge of the pond and grabbed the rope. The waterlogged raft was heavy. He pulled slowly, afraid that the raft would dip and fill with water, then sink.

The raft bumped the edge of the pond, throwing

toads from the screen onto the pile of toads scrambling from the bottom. Owen dropped the rope and grabbed the raft with both hands. He tugged it past the flashlight beam and jerked with a loud grunt. The boards scraped against the concrete, and the toads rolled backward. He pulled and grunted until half the raft had cleared the water. Then he held the left side of the raft and jerked it onto land. The raft pitched forward and knocked the flashlight into the pond.

Owen heard the splash and crept to the edge. "Darn," he whispered. He saw a spot of light wriggling up through the water. The flashlight lay on the pond bottom. Owen looked from the cylinder of light to the toad cage. He needed the light to find Buffy.

"Buffy?" He turned to the toad cage screen. "Are you in there, Buffy? Listen, Buffy. I'll get the flashlight and find you."

Owen had only been in the pond water once before. When he was little, he had ridden his tricycle too close to the edge and fallen in. It hadn't been too deep, not quite over his head, even then. He could probably touch bottom and stand up easily now.

But the water was murky. Owen edged over the side. Even though the night was hot, the pond felt icy. He inched into the green water. His feet touched bottom: slippery, slimy leaves and moss. He stretched his foot toward the light, but brought his toes down into squishy mud. Ugh! He stretched his leg out farther, felt the metal flashlight, and clamped his toes over it. Slowly he pushed the light across the bottom through the muddy leaves. His foot cramped. The pain was so sharp he shrieked, but he kept his toes curled around the light.

When the light was beneath him, he squatted to reach it. He dipped his shoulder under the water, held his breath, and ducked his head under as he grabbed for the light. He felt it slip, reached again, and caught it. Then he scrambled onto the concrete and sat shivering.

The light was still working, but its beam seemed paler. It would probably be all right once it dried out. Owen shone it onto the toads. He opened the cage door and saw white throats gleam as the toads stretched their heads toward the door.

"Buffy, I know you're in there," Owen said. He reached in and took a toad out. He saw instantly that this was not Buffy. He reached into the cage again. One by one he lifted the toads out and held them before him. He examined them, trying to find one, the only one, with three legs. When he set them down beside the pond, they hopped away.

"Go on," Owen said. He didn't want to put them back into the cage. The toads were miserable and hungry. They would probably die in there. And the raft was sinking. Richard would be mad. But Owen didn't care. He didn't care if Richard yelled at him or tried to punch him or wouldn't let him be with the other kids for the rest of his life. It wasn't his fault. It was Richard's fault for putting the toads in the cage in the first place.

His fingers wrapped around a soft glob of water-logged toad. Its legs hung down like those of a rubber frog at Woolworth's. Owen set the toad down. It lay still. He watched, hoping the toad would move, but it didn't. Owen knew the toad was dead. He was relieved to see that the toad had two hind legs.

The pond water had begun to dry on his body, and he felt itchy all over. He scratched his shoulders and legs, which made them itch more. Then he noticed that mosquitoes were buzzing around him. He wished the toads would catch a few and eat them. They were supposed to be so good at pest control. The toads didn't seem interested at all right now in pest control. Owen swatted twice, then suddenly the flashlight dimmed and went out, and he felt lost.

Owen stared, opening his eyes as wide as he could in the new-moon darkness. He had to feel each toad to see if it had front and back legs. From a mound of toads near the far corner he picked up a small wriggling toad and felt the tiny stump at the side of his body.

"Buffy! It's you."

Buffy sat calmly in the palm of his left hand. Owen cupped his right hand over Buffy and leaned close. If Buffy was in a panic, he didn't show it. He clung to Owen's hand as Owen leaned forward to kiss Buffy on the nose.

With his left foot Owen turned the cage on its side and left the top door open. He grabbed the flashlight and tiptoed back into the house. He shook the flashlight before he put it back in the kitchen drawer and went upstairs to put Buffy in the ice-cream bucket. He set the pail on his bunk and slipped his damp shorts off, leaving them on the floor where they dropped. He started to slide into bed but got up and crept back downstairs and out the back door.

Once again he stood in the darkness. Mosquitoes landed instantly on his outstretched arms, and he smacked three. He took them back to his room and dropped them into Buffy's bucket through the airholes punched in the lid.

"Good night, Buffy."

Owen wrapped his arms around the bucket and lay back. He took a deep breath and smelled the dried pond water on his body. He let out the breath with a sigh and fell asleep.

8

SNEAK!

"Owen, you sneak! I know you did it. Come on, tell me."

Owen heard angry shouting. He felt pressure on his arms. Someone was shaking him. Was he having a nightmare? He opened his eyes. Worse than a nightmare. It was Richard, leaning over his bed, gripping his arms, and yelling at him.

Suddenly Owen remembered. The toads. The pond. "Buffy!" he shouted and turned to make sure the bucket was safe beside him on the bed.

Richard reached across him to grab the bucket, but Owen wrapped his arms around it. Richard managed to rip the lid off.

"Just what I thought. You little sneak." Richard stood suddenly, clunking his head against the top bunk. "Ow!" He screamed even louder. "You stole that toad from the raft and let the toads out. You even killed one."

"No, I didn't." Owen sat up in bed, shielding the bucket with his body. "You did. And I didn't steal Buffy. He's my toad."

"You sabotaged the whole operation." Richard paused and rubbed his head. Then he held his hand out. "Give me that toad, Owen. I'm going to sell him."

"No!" Owen screamed. "No. I'll tell Mom. Mo-om!"

"Richard! Owen!" Mom stood in the doorway with an armful of towels for the laundry. "What is going on?"

"All my toads are gone, Mom," Richard said.

"But they're supposed to be gone today."

"Mom, I was going to sell them. I already had some promised. But no, Owen had to go and let them all out. Don't you see? I can't sell them now. They're gone."

Mom looked puzzled. She dropped the towels on the floor and came into the room.

"I'll have to go out and catch them all over again." Richard shook his head.

"No, Richard," Mom said firmly. "No more toads."

Richard pointed at Owen. "It's all his fault, the little sneak."

"Owen, did you really let all the toads out?" Mom asked.

Owen started to get out of bed. Then he realized he didn't have his undershorts on. He pulled the sheet to his chin and clamped it to his body with his arms.

"Owen?" Mom expected an answer.

Owen nodded.

"I told Richard to get rid of them. You should have let him do it. It was his job." Mom shrugged and looked at the ceiling. She sighed loudly, then gave each of them an exasperated look. "I want both of you to straighten up and make an effort. Now."

"I am making an effort," Richard said. "I'm trying to earn some money so I won't have to ask you for any. Fred and I have been saving up to buy bows. Dad said if I earned the money, I could get one. With the toad business we would have made enough. Owen should pay me back."

Mom shook her head. "Richard, you couldn't have sold all those toads."

"And Mom," Owen began to hope that Mom might be on his side, "the cage was filling up with water. The toads were drowning. You should have seen them. I had to save them."

"Sneak!" Richard shouted.

"Richard." Mom meant business. "If you want to earn some money, all you have to do is get out the lawn mower and start on the lawn. We always pay you for doing that chore."

"Aw, Mom. That's not fair."

"If you want to earn money, I think you'd better mow. I'm sure Fred has plenty of things to do at his home, too."

"But what am I going to tell the Ragsdales and the Steins?"

"Tell them to catch their own toads," said Mom.

Richard shook his fist at Owen. Then he said in a steely voice, "That's the last time I let you do anything with us. Ever. From now on you'd better keep your distance, Sneak."

"Richard!" Mom pointed to the doorway.

Richard kicked at the towels on the hall floor and stomped down the stairs.

"Mom, do you want to see Buffy?" Owen held up the bucket.

Mom glanced down at the bucket. "Yes, I see him. Nice," she said without enthusiasm.

He hadn't really expected Mom to be impressed with his toad. He should be happy that she didn't say anything about getting rid of Buffy. She hadn't even complained about having a wild animal in the house, which was what she had done last year in a big way when he had caught a garter snake and kept it in the clothes hamper in the hall. Mom had been even madder when the snake crawled out.

Owen always wondered where the snake had gone.

"Owen, I think you should get up and eat your breakfast. Please wash your hands first. Now I know why you slept so late. You must have been up half the night. I was afraid you were coming down with something. You can play with Elke after you eat. I have to run to the office now." She bent down to kiss Owen on the head. "Owen, I think you should try harder to get along with Richard."

"Okay." Owen knew this wasn't the moment to tell Mom it was impossible for him to get along with Richard.

After breakfast Owen carried Buffy in his bucket to the backyard. Elke was on her knees in the grass, piling up mounds of gravel she had gleaned from the alley. Owen could hear the mower engine rage at the side of the house as Richard shoved the mower across the lawn.

Elke looked up from the castle she was building with the rocks. "I heard about the toads," she said. "Richard told me. Why did you do it, anyway? He was going to let them out today."

"I had to get Buffy. You sure forgot all about him when Mom said we were going to Richard's ball game."

"I didn't forget. Richard probably would have sold him to you today."

"But he's my toad. Anyway, you should have

seen the raft. It was sinking. One of the toads is dead. If I hadn't pulled the raft out, they'd all be dead."

Elke nodded in sympathy. "I saw the dead toad."

"Do you want to help me bury it? We can have a funeral."

"Okay." Elke dropped the rock she was holding and brushed her hands together. "Richard was mad, wasn't he?"

"Real mad."

They went over to the edge of the pond where Owen had saved the toads during the night. The raft sat on the cement. Half of its flat bottom jutted out above the pond. The empty cage lay on its side. The dead toad was by the pond edge. Owen picked it up. Its body was stiff and stuck to the cement. Its white belly was smooth and firm like the tiny bars of hotel soap Dad brought back from his trips. Owen laid the toad on a maple leaf. Elke scooped up the leaf and carried it to a patch of bare ground beneath the forsythia bush at the edge of the backyard. Owen scooped out a shallow hole and Elke set the toad and leaf at the bottom.

Owen got Buffy's bucket and placed it beside the grave. "I'm sorry about your friend, Buffy. He's dead now. He's not gone, though. He'll be under this bush."

"Not for long," Elke said. "He's going to rot and turn into mud and dirt."

"Maybe we should put him in a coffin. Grandpa was in a coffin, wasn't he?"

"Sure. But it doesn't matter," Elke said, sounding like Richard. "Sooner or later, everything rots."

Owen felt a sudden sadness. He turned from the white-bellied toad to look at Buffy, who sat with one eye closed on a pile of leaves on the bottom of the bucket.

Elke bowed her head. "Ashes to ashes, dirt to dirt, and toads to mud."

"God bless the toad," Owen said. Then they both said, "Amen," and covered the toad with fistfuls of dirt patted firm with their palms. They set two stones on the mound of dirt and picked some buttercups and a fat yellow dandelion to throw on the grave.

Elke went back to her gravel castle while Owen looked for food for Buffy. He smacked mosquitoes and gnats and found a dead moth in the grass. He dropped the bugs into the bucket, but Buffy didn't notice. Owen could see that the three mosquitoes from the night feeding lay untouched. Owen picked one up and set it right on Buffy's head. Buffy sat as still as a rock.

"Buffy, you have to eat. This is good food," Owen pleaded. Finally Owen went to Elke for help.

"I saw a movie once," Elke said. "Frogs and toads like to catch live bugs. I think maybe the bugs have to move. What does it say about feeding them in your book?"

"My book doesn't talk about feeding them. It's only about wild frogs and toads, not pet ones. Isn't it hard to catch mosquitoes alive?"

"Impossible. Anyway they would just fly out of the bucket through the airholes. Maybe you could get them to come to Buffy."

"Mosquitoes don't like toads," Owen said. "They like me."

"They don't like you. They like your blood. They smell it or something, like sharks. You have to put some blood in Buffy's bucket."

"Huh?" Owen didn't like anything that had to do with cuts and scrapes and blood. When he was six, he had cut his fingers with a knife that Richard had sharpened too much. Just thinking about it made his fingers sting.

But Buffy had to eat. And Buffy had to have bugs. Owen scratched the scab over a mosquito bite on his arm. The scab came off, and a bead of blood appeared. Owen ran his finger over the blood, then smeared it on the side of the bucket. "Yuck." He squeezed more blood onto a maple leaf and set the leaf in the bucket. It hadn't hurt that much.

"That ought to work," Elke said.

Owen could hear the admiration in her voice.

He put the uncovered bucket beneath the

forsythia hedge. He crawled under the low-hanging branches and lay still. The branches scratched his head, and a squadron of mosquitoes attacked his bare legs and shoulders. Owen swatted at them and tried to concentrate on the scene in the ice-cream bucket.

He saw a couple of mosquitoes buzzing around Buffy. Then something happened. It was so quick that Owen couldn't believe he had seen it. Maybe he hadn't seen it, but Buffy's mouth had moved. He had shifted, and now there was only one mosquito buzzing around the maple leaf. Buffy was smiling, Owen thought, and his bulging eyes gleamed. For sure, Buffy had caught the mosquito. Owen felt as proud of Buffy as if that toad had been a bird dog fetching a quail.

He left Buffy under the hedge while he and Elke played with the gravel castle. Elke had set up plastic figures inside. The figures came from cupcakes Mom bought at the bakery. Owen took the clowns and cowboys. Elke played with the white horse and the ballerina. She called them Prancer and Princess Elvira.

"Go get Buffy," Elke said. "He can be Princess Elvira's pet dragon."

"Dragons aren't pets," Owen said.

"He can be a giant pet toad then."

Owen put Buffy in the middle of the gravel walls and dug a tiny pool and set grass and leaves around it.

"He likes it," Elke said.

Owen watched Buffy carefully. He just sat by the castle pond, then slowly hobbled over to a mound of freshly cut grass Owen had tossed in. Maybe Buffy did like it. He didn't try to jump out or run away.

It was almost lunchtime when Owen realized he hadn't heard the lawn mower for a while.

"I wonder where Richard is?" Owen said. It was important to keep track of Richard today. He might be mad about the toads for a long time. He might do something to get even with Owen. "I didn't see him go to Fred's."

"I saw him cross the street to go uptown," Elke said. "When he quit mowing. Don't worry. He probably got his money, and everything'll be okay."

Elke started talking about Princess Elvira. Princess Elvira was in love with Buffy, and Buffy would grow up to be a prince.

"No way, Elke." Owen touched Buffy's rough spotted back. "Buffy's going to be a toad forever."

"But Owen." Elke started to argue when a flat dark green stick plunged down beside the castle wall.

"Look, guys." Richard surprised them. He was holding the stick and bent it against his forearm to loop a leather cord from bottom to top. Richard stood tall with his shoulders back. Two yellow arrows were wedged under his belt. He pulled the string slowly, bending the bow into a half circle. Then he eased the bow back into shape.

"A hunting bow," Owen said. He had never seen such a big bow. Richard's new bow wasn't a flimsy toy to shoot rubber-tipped arrows. It was for real. Owen wondered what it would feel like to pull the string back. Would he be strong enough to do it?

"It's neat," Elke said. "Can I try?"

"No way," Richard scoffed. "I'm going to show Fred," he announced. "This is the one I wanted. I told them to hold it for me at the Sport Shop until I got the rest of the money. I didn't even need those stupid toads." He headed for the alley, then stopped. "You owe me a dollar, Sneak," he said to Owen.

"No I don't," Owen yelled as Richard swaggered up the alley. "I'll never pay you anything." His anger burst from him in one big scream. "And toads aren't stupid!"

Owen crouched, ready to run in case Richard plucked an arrow from his belt and shot at him with his powerful new bow.

9
A SAFE PLACE

Owen didn't see Richard the rest of the day, but he kept Buffy close to him just in case. When he went to the bathroom, he took Buffy and locked the door. When he sat and read on the upstairs porch, Buffy was beside him. When he ate supper, he set the bucket under the table in front of his chair and rested his feet on it. It was the only way to keep Buffy safe after what they had been through. Just because Richard wasn't around didn't mean he had forgotten. He could be thinking up ways to get even.

That evening Richard ate supper at Fred's. He even slept over, which put Owen in a good mood. Mom was a lot more cheerful, too, compared with her angry mood in the morning. When Owen went to bed and Mom came into his room to say good night, she didn't tell him Buffy's bucket had to be outside instead of sitting on the bed beside him.

"Owen, I have to work at a League rummage sale tomorrow. When you get up, go on over to Grandma Snyder's for cinnamon rolls. She's expecting you."

"Yum," Owen said. He couldn't wait. Grandma made the best cinnamon rolls he had ever tasted. That wasn't the only reason he wanted to go. He wanted to show Buffy to Grandma, too.

Mom leaned over his bed and kissed him on the cheek. Then she tousled his hair. "It looks like you've calmed down since this morning."

"You, too, Mom."

Mom smiled. "I thought you two were going to bring the walls down, shouting and carrying on like that." She shook her head. "You and Richard don't agree about things, I know. Richard is a lot older than you, and besides, you're very different from each other. But the least you could both do is learn to say 'I'm sorry.' "

Owen looked up at Mom. "I can't, Mom," he said. "I'm not sorry."

Mom sighed.

"Tell Richard to say he's sorry," Owen added because he saw she was disappointed. He couldn't help it. He was telling her the truth.

"I already did," Mom said as she turned out the light.

*   *   *

The next morning Owen awoke, propped himself up on his elbow, and peered into Buffy's bucket. "Don't toads ever sleep?" he said. Since it didn't look as if Buffy could hop out, Owen had decided to leave the lid off. That way Buffy would get more air.

Buffy blinked suddenly. "Yeah, well, good morning to you, too." Owen touched Buffy. His back was cool and dry. Buffy didn't flinch or move. There was something about the way the toad sat there, comfortable with Owen's finger stroking his back, that made Owen think Buffy was grateful—grateful at having been saved and grateful at being protected by Owen.

Owen got up and dressed quickly, thinking about Grandma's cinnamon rolls.

He hurried out the back door, with Buffy jostling gently in his bucket.

"Look!" Owen called out as he reached the top of the stairs at Grandma's. He could smell the cozy welcome of cinnamon and butter and baking bread.

"In here, Owen." Grandma was sitting at the narrow table by the kitchen window. "Have you had your breakfast yet?"

Owen shook his head.

She set her teacup down and asked, "What do you want to show me? It must be important."

Owen thrust the bucket toward Grandma. "I call him Buffy."

Grandma peered into the bucket. "Toads before breakfast. Don't you think that's a bit much?" She studied Buffy for a moment. "He's a fine toad, but a little unusual."

"I know. What do you think happened to his leg?"

Grandma shook her head. "Hard to say."

"I caught him at the cemetery, right by Grandpa's grave."

"A good place. I expect that's where you'll let him go."

Owen didn't answer. He hadn't thought about letting Buffy go. He wanted to keep him.

"For now you can put your toad right here by the table. Now wash your hands and have yourself a fresh-from-the-oven cinnamon roll."

"Yum!" Owen set Buffy on the floor. He washed up and scooted onto the wooden chair across from Grandma.

Owen bit into the roll, chewed its soft sweetness, then set it down and licked melted brown sugar from his fingers.

"So what did you do yesterday? Your mother told me this morning there was a bit of excitement," Grandma said.

Owen explained about the toad raft and how he had to save Buffy and that Richard and Fred had been mean to the toads. "One toad died," he said, "and me and Elke buried him."

"Richard should have been more careful," she said. "Creatures are fragile. I think it must be an especially hard life for toads on this earth. Think of it: all the cars, bikes, and dogs."

And Richard, Owen thought. If Richard had kept those toads any longer, Owen would have had to bury more than one.

"Grandma, did Grandpa rot?"

Grandma set her teacup down, frowning. "Who told you that?"

"Elke. When we buried the toad. She told me it wouldn't stay there. It'd rot and turn to dirt. And she said that's what happened to Grandpa."

"Oh, that Elke." Grandma sighed. "I suppose, to be honest, that's one way to say it. 'Decay' is another, or 'decompose.' You know how the weeds and potato peels we put on my compost pile turn to dirt?"

Owen nodded. He thought about how the big, fenced-in pile got smaller even after you piled things on top of it. Then after a while the bottom of the pile turned to dirt, and Grandma raked it out and put it on the garden.

"Grandpa's bones and body will do much the same."

"But wasn't he in a coffin?"

"Yes. But that was eight years ago. I suppose a coffin makes it take longer. But Owen, there was more to Grandpa than his bones. His body is gone, but he is still with me, with us. I remember him. I remember him to you when I tell you about him."

"It's not the same," Owen said. "I wish Grandpa were here. I wish I could remember him."

"I wish you could, too," said Grandma.

Owen finished his roll and drank a cup of milk. Then he got up to go. Taking Buffy's bucket by the handle, he said, "I don't want Buffy to die. I want Buffy to live forever."

Grandma followed him to the stairway that led down to the front door. "Owen, Elke is playing with Lucy. Uncle Homer is bringing her back when he comes to take me to the eye doctor's. Your mother said to call Richard if you need anything. He's at Fred's."

No way, Owen thought. He would dial 911 before he'd call Richard for anything.

When Owen got home, he took Buffy up to the open porch. He wanted to go up there to think. Also, he had seen some ants by the geranium planter. Maybe he would catch some for Buffy. Ants are flimsy, though. It would be hard to catch them without squishing them.

The key wasn't in the porch door. Owen dropped to his knees to look. He couldn't find it anywhere. When he reached up and turned the knob, the door opened. He didn't need the key. But Owen was sure he had put the key back yesterday when he was up here.

Owen sat down near the wall of the house and let his feet hang over the balcony edge in the sunlight. He set Buffy's bucket behind him and shoved it into the shadow of the roof. He didn't want Buffy to overheat.

Owen reached back to pick up the watering can. Good. It still had water in it. He drizzled streams of water over the red geraniums Mom had put in the planters along the railing. Then he stood up to water the pot of ivy hanging from the ceiling. Taking care of the plants was his job. Mom almost never came to the balcony. Owen put the can back, sat down in front of the railing, and looked out over the neighborhood.

Richard and Fred appeared suddenly in the alley. Richard carried his green bow at his right side. His hand clutched the bow and an arrow that was notched onto the bowstring. Richard looked up, then quickly turned to say something to Fred. Owen was sure Richard had seen him.

Owen waited for them to come up the back steps and into the kitchen, but they kept on going down the alley. Maybe they were going in the front door. Owen listened for their voices. If Richard and Fred were in the house, they'd go to the kitchen. When Mom wasn't home, sometimes Richard and Fred took the ice cream from the freezer and ate right out of the bucket with a spoon. And they never let Owen have any. If they were in the kitchen, they must have been holding their breath. Owen couldn't hear a sound. Maybe they had stayed on the front porch and were sitting in the swing there.

Owen had the uncomfortable feeling that they

were talking about him. Richard had to be mad at him, for sure, which meant Fred was mad at him, too. They had probably told Matthew and Mark and Patrick and made it look as if it had been his fault. Everyone in the neighborhood but Elke would be mad at him.

The back door squealed open, then slammed. Owen snapped forward over the railing and looked downward.

Fred ambled out onto the patio beneath the porch. "Hey, Owen! How would you like for Buffy to be famous?"

"What are you talking about?"

"We're doing scientific experiments. We want Buffy to be the first airborne toad. We're going to launch him on an arrow."

"No, you're not!" cried Owen. "I'll never let you."

"There are risks," Fred said, as if he hadn't heard Owen. "You know how dangerous flying in space is. And he might not make it. But we can tie him on pretty good. Anyway, we need a toad, and since you let them all go . . ."

Owen slipped his legs from the slats. "You can't have Buffy." He turned around to grab Buffy's bucket just as the porch door slammed shut. The bucket was gone. Owen jumped up and ran to the door. He tried to push it open. He could see Richard through the sheer window curtain, and he could hear the key clicking in the lock.

Then Richard was gone. They had planned to steal Buffy. While Fred had been talking to Owen, Richard had sneaked upstairs. Owen turned the knob and banged his shoulder against the door.

"Richard! Open up. Open the door. Give me Buffy!" Owen beat the door with his fists until they ached. Then he ran back to the railing. Richard was carrying his long green bow and Buffy's bucket.

"Richard! Ri-chard!" Owen screamed. "You'd better not hurt Buffy. Or I'll . . ." Owen was so mad he didn't know what he would do. "I'll throw your mitt in the pond," he hollered. "I'll break your bow and all your arrows."

"Yeah, we're really afraid," Fred shouted back.

Richard cupped his hands around his mouth. "Relax, Owen. Buffy's going to be famous." He nudged Fred. They turned and trotted up the alley.

Owen stared at them until they disappeared around the corner of Fred's garage. They would go to the empty lot next door to Fred's. Owen was sure.

Why had he let it happen? All the time he had known Richard would get even. He would take Buffy and do something mean to him. Richard had planned it all along, and Owen had done nothing. He was just a helpless kid who couldn't stand up to his big brother.

"I hate you, Richard," he said. Then he punched the railing and screamed at the empty alley. "I hate you!"

10

RESCUE ATTEMPT

"Please, God, don't let anything happen to Buffy."
Owen's voice cracked. He sure hoped God heard him.
No one else in the neighborhood had.

Owen looked down at the patio bricks and the
cherry tree. It was too far to jump. He'd smash himself if he even tried. He wished right then that he
could fly. Maybe he could want it bad enough for it to
happen.

He shook his head. That's stupid, he thought.
People can't fly. What he needed was for Mom to
come home and open the door somehow. Maybe she
had an extra key. Or for Dad to pull up in the driveway a month early, just like that, in the middle of the
day. Dad could set his tall painting ladder against the
railing, and Owen could climb down and run off and
stop Richard. And he could stop him too, by himself.
He just needed help to get down.

Owen leaned his stomach against the railing. No one would come. He was alone, stuck on the balcony porch. Tears gummed his eyes. He blinked and swallowed. To keep from crying, he focused his stare on the rusted drainpipe at the corner of the porch. He noticed that it went from the roof above to the patio where it drained into the roots of the cherry tree. Suddenly it became clear. I can do it, he told himself. I can get down if I can reach the drainpipe.

He gripped the railing and swung his leg over it. Step by step Owen edged toward the drainpipe. He tried not to think about the hard patio bricks far below him. He forced from his mind the thought of falling. As soon as he was near enough, he reached out and grabbed the drainpipe with both hands. It was too wide to get a good grip on.

He straddled the pipe and inched his way down, bumping his knees against the rough bricks of the house wall. His hands began to ache. His knees stung. But what did his scraped knees matter when at this very minute Buffy could be tied onto the end of an arrow and shot into space? He gripped the drainpipe tighter.

To keep from slipping, Owen pushed his toes against the house. Easy. Easy. The drainpipe creaked and began to pull away. Owen felt a jabbing pain below his right knee just as he reached out to grab a branch of the cherry tree. Something sharp on the pipe must have cut him. He looked down—for an instant—at the red gash spreading on his leg. Then the drainpipe tore free from the house. He reached out and gripped the branch with his right hand, letting go of the pipe with his left. Dangling, he swung to the tree and climbed down, shaking blossoms like snow onto the patio. From a low branch he dropped to his feet, lost his balance, and sat down hard. He jumped up quickly, brushed dirt off his tingling hands, and ran up the alley.

"Richard! Richard!" he screamed. "Don't you hurt Buffy!"

His chest pounded as he ran past the garage and stared at the overgrown lot.

Richard was pulling back on an arrow notched in his bowstring. He released it. The arrow flew up and arched over the plum tree. It descended like a missile, headfirst into the earth.

Was Buffy on that arrow?

"Buffy!" Owen screamed. He charged at Richard.

"Owen!" Fred shouted.

Richard turned just as Owen plowed into him. Richard dropped his bow as they both toppled over. Owen pounded Richard with his fists, but Richard grabbed Owen's arms and shoved him onto his back. Fred pinned him down, and Richard got up.

"Are you crazy? How did you—" Richard

dropped to his knees and put his hand on Owen's leg. "Good grief, Owen. What did you do to yourself?"

Fred let go of Owen's arms.

"Your leg, you goofball. Can't you feel it?"

Owen raised up on his elbow and looked at the blood-smeared gash on his right leg. From below his knee to midcalf an ugly blotch spread out. There was blood on his shorts and blood on his socks. But he could hardly feel it, almost as if his leg belonged to someone else. He looked away quickly.

Richard tore his baseball T-shirt off and tied it around Owen's leg above the cut. Owen felt Richard grab his shoulders and raise him to his feet. "We've got to get you to Dr. Fulham's. Fred, where's your old wagon? We'll wheel him up to the Main Street Clinic."

"In the garage," Fred said, then ran toward his house.

"But Buffy," Owen protested. "I'm not leaving Buffy."

Richard wouldn't let him go. "What were you doing, Owen? How'd you get down?"

"I climbed. I had to." Owen felt mad all over again. He was right to be mad. Owen looked into Richard's brown eyes. "You locked the door."

Richard looked down. He didn't say anything. Then Fred ran up with the wagon.

"Good, Fred. Help me put him in the wagon."

Richard lifted Owen from under his arms, and Fred took his feet. "Careful," Richard cautioned as they set him down easy. Richard took the handle and tugged the wagon into motion. Fred trotted beside him.

Owen grabbed the sides of the wagon as he bounced in misery the six blocks to the clinic. His leg began to hurt again, but what hurt more was the ache in his throat. What had happened to Buffy? If Richard had killed Buffy . . .

At the emergency-room door Richard said to Fred, "You can go back now, but get my bow." Then he added, "Check on the toad, will you, Fred?"

Richard pulled the wagon right into the emergency room. He stopped in front of a big, redheaded nurse. "It's my brother, Owen. He has a bad cut."

Owen heard him whisper. "I think he'll need stitches—and a tetanus shot."

Not stitches. Not a shot. Owen gripped the edge of the wagon. He hated shots. He tried to climb out. "No shots," he said.

The nurse picked him up under the armpits. "You were right to bring Owen in. How did you say he cut his leg?" She set Owen on the examination table.

"Oh, he was just playing outside, you know, around some old sharp, rusty metal, or something."

"No, I wasn't—" Owen stopped short when

Richard bumped the examination table. He looked at Richard. Richard glared back. His eyes told Owen not to say another word.

"Is your mother at work? Did she send you here?" the nurse asked.

"She's not home right now. She's helping at a rummage sale," Richard answered. "Somewhere."

"Do you have her number? I'll have the receptionist call."

Richard stared blankly at Owen. "What's her number? I forgot where she was going to be."

Owen shook his head. Why did they have to have a phone number to fix his leg? Why didn't they just put medicine on it and let him go home? If they couldn't phone Mom, would they let him go home anyway? He could put a Band-Aid on it himself.

"Your father?" the nurse asked.

"He's out of town," Richard said. "Can't you just stitch it up?"

"Stitch!" Owen whined.

"We really need to talk to a grown-up first."

Grandma, Owen thought. She would help him out of this mess. She wouldn't let them stitch him up. "Call Grandma. She's a grown-up," he said. "Her number is 555-5982."

"Thank you." The nurse noted the number on a card she pulled from her pocket. Then she slid Owen farther back on the table so that his legs stuck out in front of him. "Hmm, I see," she murmured. "I'll be right back to clean this cut up for Dr. Fulham to look at."

"No stitches, Richard. I don't want stitches." Owen wished he could jump down and run away.

Richard grabbed Owen's shoulder and squeezed. "It'll be okay. You'll see. How are you doing?"

"My butt hurts," Owen said. "That was a bumpy ride."

"I mean your leg, Owen."

"It stings. A lot."

"Look, Grandma is going to come," Richard said brusquely. "Will you promise not to tell her what happened? I mean, if you tell, we'll both be in BIG trouble."

"But you'll be in bigger trouble," Owen said. "It was your fault."

Richard frowned. He looked jumpy. He even acted scared, Owen thought. He had never seen Richard scared before, but he knew enough about being scared to know when he was looking at it. And he knew what kind of scared it was, too. Richard had done something wrong, very wrong. If Owen told, Richard would be in big trouble. Mom would punish him. She would ground him for a year and make him clean both bathrooms and the basement. She would make him clear the cobwebs from the fruit cellar and get rid of all the spiders, too. She would probably take his new bow away—forever.

That's why Richard stood there, pleading for Owen not to say anything. It gave Owen a strange feeling. He could say the words to get Richard in trouble, or he could keep quiet and everything would be the same. Except for one thing.

"Okay," Owen said. "I'll keep it secret." Secret, he thought. The first secret ever between him and Richard. And that was the difference.

Richard tousled his hair. "Thanks."

"Unless you hurt Buffy." Owen's voice was dead serious. He wanted Richard to know that he meant it. "If anything happens to Buffy, I'll tell everyone everything."

"Don't worry. The toad's okay. I sent Fred after him."

The nurse bustled back into the room. Owen noticed a bottle and a blob of cotton on the tray she carried.

"Your grandma's on her way. And you're going to be as right as rain in no time," the nurse said cheerfully.

"Yikes!" Owen winced when she pressed the antiseptic-soaked cotton onto his cut. "Ow! Ow!" He sniffed and blinked to keep his eyes and nose from running.

"There. That looks much better."

"Hello, boys." Dr. Fulham marched into the

room, washed her hands at the sink, and came to Owen's side to examine his leg. She studied the gash in silence, then nodded to the nurse.

"Got into something sharp and rusty, I see," she said. Her brown eyes widened in sympathy. She moved Owen's leg gently. "I'll be right back to take care of you."

Owen took a deep breath. He looked at Richard, who nodded and held his hands up to calm him. Owen felt queasy inside, but he tried to look brave.

Dr. Fulham hurried back into the room, stretching a pair of rubber gloves over her fingers.

"This may sting a little. But only for a moment, I guarantee." Her voice was soothing. Her grip on Owen's leg was firm.

Owen stiffened. He felt Richard clench his shoulder again. This time Richard didn't let go. Dr. Fulham took a long syringe from the nurse and aimed it at Owen's leg. "Take a deep breath. Now relax."

Owen tightened every muscle in his body. "No. No."

Owen closed his eyes. He couldn't even breathe. He felt Richard's fingers grip his shoulder. It was a good feeling, a safe feeling. He would be all right if Richard held on. Then the bee sting of the needle pinched his leg. "Ow." He began to breathe hard. "Ouch. OOOO." Suddenly Richard let go of his shoulder.

Owen opened his eyes and saw Richard sink to the floor.

"He's fainted," Dr. Fulham said calmly. "Nurse Jackson, can you help this boy?"

Owen didn't know what to think. His leg felt mushy, then thick and heavy. No pain. He watched Nurse Jackson revive Richard and lift him to a sitting position.

"Let me take you out to a nice comfortable sofa in the next room. You'll feel better in a jiffy."

"No!" Owen screamed. The sound of his voice surprised him. He felt everyone stare at him. They wanted to know what had caused him to scream.

"He's my brother," Owen explained. "I want him to stay here."

Richard half crawled to the chair beside the desk in the corner. He sat in it and looked at Owen. His lips were pinched tightly together. His face was ghost white. He opened his mouth and sucked a breath of air. "I'm going to stay here," he said.

For the first time he could remember, Owen felt like grabbing Richard and hugging him.

11

THE SECRET

Owen clung to Richard as he hopped into the clinic waiting room.

"Grandma!" he said. "Why did you let them give me stitches?"

Grandma looked up. So did Uncle Homer. And Matthew, Mark, Lucy, and Joanne. They had all come. Owen sighed. He really hadn't expected a family gathering. He didn't feel like a party. All he wanted was to go home and find Buffy and go to his room and sleep.

Grandma bustled up to Owen and eyed the bandage on his leg, hugging him away from Richard. "You needed them, Owen," she said. "You're going to be all right. Uncle Homer brought me as soon as Nurse Jackson called. I couldn't see to walk."

"Why are you wearing sunglasses?" Owen asked.

She raised her sunglasses, and Owen saw that

her gray eyes were almost black. "My pupils are still dilated. From the eye doctor's."

"It looks funny, Grandma. You look like someone else."

Uncle Homer picked Owen up and carried him outside to the blue pickup truck parked out front.

"How'd you do it?" Matthew asked.

"Was there a lot of blood?" Mark said.

"Yeah. It ran all over his leg," Richard answered.

"Don't be gross, you guys." Lucy glared at Richard. Then she turned to Owen, and her face became worried and sympathetic.

"Elke's here, too," Joanne said. "But Uncle Homer wouldn't let her go in the clinic."

Elke was sitting in the front seat of the truck. She scooted over when Uncle Homer opened the door and set Owen beside her.

"Buffy!" Owen reached for the bucket on Elke's lap.

"Oh, that toad." Grandma eased up onto the seat beside Owen. "He's in better shape than you are."

"What happened, anyway?" Elke asked. "Fred said it was an accident."

Owen didn't answer. "Is he all right? Is he all right?" He fumbled at the plastic lid. Finally Elke helped him tear it off.

Buffy sat motionless on a little pile of pebbles and dirt. Owen held his breath as he watched for the mottled skin above Buffy's stomach to move. Very slightly it moved in and out, in and out. Owen shifted the bucket to his lap and stuck his hand in to stroke Buffy.

"He feels warm."

"It's kind of hot out here in the truck," Elke said. "But Fred said I had to bring him. He said Richard would be mad if I didn't."

A thump sounded on the back window. Elke reached up and thumped back. Owen held the bucket up and grinned at the cousins and Richard, who clustered around the rear window peeking in. Richard nodded.

"Sit down back there!" Uncle Homer ordered. Then he started the truck.

Owen held Buffy in the palm of his hand all the way home.

All of the family sat in the living room with Owen. He hadn't moved from the sofa where Uncle Homer had laid him. He was drinking lemonade that Grandma had made. Warm lemonade, because she had used most of the ice for the pack she had placed on his leg.

Although he was not in the mood for a family party, Owen was grateful that Uncle Homer began to tell stories. Accident stories. The stories he told, everyone knew by heart. First, how the lawn mower had clipped off the tip of his little finger. Then he talked about Lucy's crash on a two-wheeler when she was six. "Turned her two front teeth black, what was left of them, and then they fell out," he said.

"Oh, Dad," Lucy groaned.

Owen waited for Uncle Homer to tell about the time Mark got his leg stuck in the boardwalk at a Fourth of July picnic. Owen didn't mind the stories. As long as Uncle Homer talked, no one mentioned his leg or asked what had happened to it. That was one thing he didn't want to discuss.

Then Mom came home.

"Owen, what on earth happened to your leg?" She hurried to the sofa and sat down beside him.

"Don't scrunch me, Mom." Owen leaned away from her. "It hurts." His leg didn't really hurt. It was still heavy and numb. But Owen was afraid that if Mom hugged him or even touched him, he would cry.

Mom brushed his hair from his forehead. "Poor Owen," she said. "It must have hurt a lot. But you'll be all right now."

She laid her hand on his forehead. Owen felt tears run down his cheeks, and there he was, doing just what he didn't want to, crying in front of everyone.

"But what happened?" Mom asked. She pulled a tissue from her jeans pocket and wiped Owen's tears.

Owen sniffed, then looked at Richard, who

stared right back at him. If Richard hadn't wanted him to tell Grandma, Richard sure wouldn't want him to say a word to anyone else, especially not Mom.

"It was an accident. I was hanging from the tree branch and dropped down on something sharp."

"From the cherry tree?"

Owen nodded.

"I think you should stay out of trees, Owen."

"I was up the alley," Richard said. "I heard Owen screaming and I came. All I saw was a piece of gutter. It must have come off the side of the house sometime, Mom."

"I'll take care of that for you, Lila," Uncle Homer said. "Just keep the kids away from it."

"Amen!" Mom agreed. "You heard your uncle, kids."

Grandma got up. "How about sandwiches? I was just puttering around the kitchen a minute ago."

"Sounds great," Mom said. "Are you hungry, dear?" she asked Owen.

He shook his head, and she bent over and kissed him. "Maybe you should rest."

Owen slept through the sandwiches. He slept through Buffy's meal, too. Elke woke him when she set Buffy's bucket beside him on the sofa. "The mosquitoes are thick under the hedge. I'm pretty sure Buffy ate some."

"Thanks, Elke."

"Guess what. Dad just called. Mom's talking to him now. I got to talk, too. I told him about your accident. And I told Dad you have a pet. But I didn't say what it is."

"I want to talk to him, too."

Elke helped Owen get up and hobble into the hallway. Mom sat at the telephone table. She smiled. "Here he is, Ralph. A little sleepy, but all in one piece."

"Hi, Tiger." Dad's voice sounded cheerful. "I hear you got hurt today."

"Hi, Dad. It was just an accident. I'm okay now."

"You're lucky Richard was around to take you to the doctor's. He told me he cleared the broken drainpipe away with Uncle Homer."

"He did? I guess I was asleep." Owen was surprised that Richard had made himself sound like a hero. What if Owen told Dad what had really happened? Would Dad believe him or Richard? If Dad ever found out the truth, he would be mad at Richard. He would be mad at Owen, too, if he knew that Owen had pulled the drainpipe off.

"You be careful now in case something else gets in your way. Don't give your mother any more worries."

"I'll try."

"What's this pet Elke told me about?"

"I found him, Dad. He's a toad. His name is Buffy."

"A toad? Toads are wild animals."

"They're amphibians, Dad. And Buffy's practically tame. He only has three legs. Something happened to one of them."

"Strange. Well, you take care he doesn't lose any more. You either, Owen. Bye, now. You can put Mom back on."

"Bye, Dad." He handed the phone to Mom and noticed Richard standing in the kitchen doorway.

Richard nodded to him. He had been listening. Well, he could relax. Owen hadn't told Dad. If Richard could read Owen's mind, he would know that Owen had wanted to tell Dad—so that Richard would be punished, not just for Buffy, but for all the mean things Richard had ever done to him. But Owen had kept quiet. That's all Richard knew.

Richard helped Owen back to the sofa. "When your leg's better, do you want to learn how to shoot my bow?" He propped Owen's leg on a pillow.

Was Richard making a joke? Owen watched him for a moment to see if he grinned or burst out laughing. If Richard was pretending, he was doing a great job.

"You mean—your new bow?"

"Yeah. What's the matter? Don't you want to try?"

Richard meant it. He was serious. He was going to let Owen shoot his bow. "Sure I want to. I can do it, too. You'll see."

"Maybe you can." Richard shrugged. "It's not so easy. You'll never do it if you give up the way you usually do."

"I won't give up."

"Anyway, you didn't act like a baby today. You didn't go and tell everyone. Maybe you've changed."

Owen's leg started throbbing harder. He closed his eyes and took a deep breath. Changed, he thought. Maybe Richard's the one who has changed.

12

THROUGH A TOAD'S EYES

Owen looked up at Nurse Jackson's chinless, white throat. It wobbled as she talked. "You'll be fine. You'll be fine," she repeated. "You'll be fine. You'll be fine."

Then Owen was no longer in the doctor's office. He was wandering through a wide field. The field had just been mowed, and Owen noticed stones, some white, some broken and dirty gray, all across the field. A cemetery. As he walked, the headstones began to grow. Or was he shrinking? The grass looked like tall reeds. The earth trembled, and he felt scared. He knew he had to find a place to hide.

Suddenly a giant foot rose above his head and crashed to the ground beside him. Owen ran as fast as he could. The earth trembled around him. Panic made him run faster, so fast he didn't know where he was going. Suddenly he ran into a wall. The wall closed around him and scooped him up. Then the wall opened, and he was sitting in a giant's hand. Owen looked up at the giant. The giant was smiling. His gray eyes looked friendly. Owen had seen those eyes before.

"Grandpa," Owen said. "You're so big."

Grandpa laughed. "In time you will be as big as I am. While you are little, don't be afraid, Owen. I'll help you."

Owen felt warm and safe in Grandpa's hand. Then Grandpa set him down beside a gravestone as tall as a skyscraper.

"I must go now," Grandpa said. He climbed into a deep cavern in front of the stone.

Owen stood alone in the tall grass. "Come back," he called, and walked to the edge. As he leaned over to look down, he lost his balance and fell, twisting and spinning. Everything was dark. He couldn't see Grandpa.

"Help!" he cried out. "Grandpa! Help me!"

"Owen! Wake up! Wake up! You're having a nightmare."

Owen opened his eyes. He saw the bunk-bed springs overhead and realized he was home in his bed. Then he saw Richard looking right at him.

"I was real tiny, Richard. And I saw a giant. It was Grandpa. I saw Grandpa."

"It was a dream, Owen."

"Grandpa's a giant."

"Grandpa's dead." Richard shook his head. "And you're awake now. You want a glass of water?"

"Yeah."

Richard headed toward the hall.

"Richard," Owen whispered loudly. "I don't like bathroom water. Can you get me kitchen water?"

The hall was dark and quiet. Owen waited for Richard to complain.

"Whatever," Richard said.

Owen listened to the stairs creak as Richard went down to the kitchen.

13
NO TOADS ALLOWED

Two days after his accident, Owen was sitting in the red wagon. He felt better. His stitches still pulled and itched, but he was getting used to them. He hadn't thought he would ever sit in the red wagon again— not after bumping his butt sore on the way to the clinic. But here he was, clunking along, with Buffy in his bucket beside him, as Richard pulled them up the sidewalk to the Carnegie Library four blocks away.

"I thought you were going to take me bow shooting today," Owen said.

"I will. When Mom gets home. I can't use my bow unless she's home. Dad said."

Elke, who was trudging ahead, turned around and frowned at them. "I don't see why we can't go swimming. Whenever Mom works all afternoon, we always go swimming."

"We can't," Richard said. "Owen has stitches."

"I don't get it." Elke was going to argue. "I don't have any stitches. You don't have any stitches. We could go, and Owen could sit on the bench and watch."

"Think about it," Richard said. "It wouldn't be fair. How would you like to go to the pool and just sit and watch?"

"I wouldn't. But I don't have to because I don't have stitches."

"Quit being so difficult." Richard stopped and scowled at Elke. The wagon bumped against his leg and jolted Owen.

"Be careful." Owen grasped the toad bucket tighter. "You're going to make Buffy carsick."

Richard was too involved in arguing with Elke to pay attention to Buffy. "Elke, we're going to the library. Mom put *me* in charge. And Owen told Mom he wants to go to the library. So that's that."

"Since when do you do what Owen wants to do?" Elke stomped up the two front steps to the library and swung open the door to go in.

Richard didn't bother to answer. Owen knew why. When Elke started talking like that, it was impossible to win an argument with her. No matter what you said, she would come up with the last word.

Maybe Richard would rather go to the pool, just as Elke said. He usually didn't do things he didn't want to do. Still, Owen knew why Richard was taking him to the library to look for more toad books. For the same reason he was going to teach Owen to shoot his bow. It was because of their secret. The secret had become a pact between him and Richard. Owen wouldn't tell, and Richard would never hurt Buffy. Richard was even trying to be nice to Owen and include him in a way he had never done before.

Elke might understand if he told her. But she might tell Mom, and Richard would be in trouble. Usually that's what Owen wanted to happen, but not this time. He wasn't going to tell anyone. Because of the pact.

Richard helped Owen get out of the wagon and hobble up the steps to the front door. Owen waited for him to get the wagon and sat back in it as soon as they went inside.

Mrs. Freiburger, the librarian, stared at them over her reading glasses. Owen slid the bucket behind him. He doubted it would do any good. Mrs. Freiburger's piercing stare could probably see right through him.

"Hello, Richard. Hello, Owen. Maybe you two should leave the red wagon outside today."

"I can't, Mrs. Freiburger. My brother's got a hurt leg. He can't walk."

Owen pointed to the bandage on his leg.

"That's too bad, Owen. I'm sorry about your leg." Mrs. Freiburger didn't sound totally convinced.

Owen thought that she might come out from behind the desk and use her X-ray vision to see through the bandage on his leg. But Mrs. Freiburger didn't move.

Finally she said, "All right, Richard. I'll let you. But please park the wagon someplace. Don't pull it between the bookshelves. And I do hope this is not some sort of trick. You have such a flair for drama. I haven't forgotten our Halloween party last year when you dressed up like Dracula and told vampire stories to the first-graders. I had so many complaints, I thought I would lose my job." She picked up the phone, which had just begun to ring.

"Richard's not making it up," Owen said. "I have stitches, Mrs. Freiburger."

The librarian dismissed them with a wave, and Richard wheeled Owen toward the juvenile books.

"Over there," Owen pointed. "Toad books are in the shelf by the drinking fountain."

Richard pulled the wagon toward the shelf—past the fairy tales and fantasy books where Elke sat reading with a stack of books by her side.

Owen noticed books on insects and butterflies. The toad books should be around here somewhere. "Stop!" Owen yelled.

"Shhh," Richard said. "Want to get kicked out?"

"No," Owen mumbled. He studied the shelf, but he couldn't find the books. The reptile and amphibian books were always there. Right before the furry animals. Right after birds.

"They're not there," Owen said, disappointed. "Somebody must have checked out all five of them. That's so greedy. Why would they take all of them?"

"You do sometimes," Richard said.

"But I don't keep them forever. Now what am I going to do?"

"What do you want to read about anyway? I figured you knew everything about toads."

"No, I don't. I want to find out what they do all winter. I mean, where they go and what they eat."

"How about the encyclopedia?"

Owen shook his head. He didn't like the encyclopedia. The volumes were big and old and had tiny print and only little black-and-white pictures. Anything but the encyclopedia. "The grown-up books, Richard. We could look at them."

"I can't wheel you over there. Mrs. Freiburger's going to say something."

"She's probably still on the phone."

"No, Owen, you wait here, and I'll bring the books back. So what are the numbers for toad books?"

"I don't know," Owen said. "There aren't any toad books here. Remember?"

Richard shrugged and studied the books on the shelf. "Okay, around 500. I'll be right back."

He lunged away like a spy on a secret mission.

Owen sat and waited. He looked at the rows of books in front of him. He turned and looked at the rows of books behind him. He didn't want a butterfly book. He had already read the dinosaur book a thousand times. He wanted a toad book.

"Why is Richard taking so long?" he whispered to Buffy. "He couldn't get lost. This library is too small."

If Owen could just push the wagon to the end of the shelf, he could see Richard on the other side of the library. Or maybe he could stand up and see over the shelves. Standing up would be easier. Owen pulled himself up by clinging to the edge of the bookshelf. He could see Mrs. Freiburger helping an old lady at the desk. He could see a man reading a newspaper near the grown-up books. He thought he saw Richard's green-striped shirt, but whoever it was moved out of sight.

Owen sat down. This was getting so boring. How long did he have to wait anyway? He stood up again, with his weight on his good leg, and pushed hard against the shelf. The wagon moved. Owen teetered, sat down, and coasted three feet to the end of the shelf.

"Elke," he whispered loudly. "Elke, come here."

Elke appeared from around the next shelf. She was holding a thick book with a dragon and a princess on the cover. "What's wrong, Owen?"

"Can you take me to the grown-up books? Richard went there, and I think he forgot about me."

"I heard Mrs. Freiburger when you came in. She'll get mad if I pull you around."

"She won't see us."

Elke set her book down and looked over her shoulder at Mrs. Freiburger. "How am I supposed to drag the wagon in front of her without her seeing me?"

Owen knew he could count on Elke to help. She liked a challenge. "We could go under the desk," he said.

"You mean, just sneak around the counter?" She hesitated, then ran behind Owen. "I've got it. Sit down. Hold the handle. You steer and I'll push."

Owen grabbed the handle and moved in his wagon across the carpeted floor.

Elke was on her knees. She groaned. "This is hard to push on the rug. You're heavy."

"It'll be easier when we get to the front desk. The floor is slick there." Elke held the wagon when they reached the alphabet-book shelf shielding them from the desk. "We'll wait till she's through helping that lady."

As soon as the woman left, Mrs. Freiburger turned to her computer monitor, and Elke gripped the back rim of the wagon and pushed. A little clunking noise and a squeak from the handle sounded as Owen tried to steer. They were right under the desk counter. Mrs. Freiburger couldn't see them now. Elke pushed harder and the wagon glided faster on the smooth wood floor. Too fast for Elke to keep up. Owen turned and saw her lose her balance and fall forward onto the floor.

Nothing held the wagon back. That last shove propelled Owen toward the tall bookshelf right in front of him. He pulled the handle to the left and the wagon lunged right. He missed the shelf and headed down the aisle—right toward Richard, who was carrying a stack of books. Richard yelled and dropped the books just as the wagon ran into him and tipped over. The jolt knocked him to his knees. Owen and the ice-cream bucket toppled onto the floor.

Richard sat in the center of the aisle, yelling at Owen for being stupid. Owen rubbed his shoulder. Then he got up quickly to a squat on his good leg. He hop-crawled toward the bucket, which was perched on its side. Buffy was gone. Owen crawled frantically around the books looking for his toad.

"Richard, I did ask you to park that wagon." Mrs. Freiburger stood at the end of the aisle. "What is going on here?"

"An accident. It was all an accident," Richard said. "I can explain."

"Buffy!" Owen reached out to cover Buffy with his palm. The toad sat unharmed under a protruding shelf.

"Buffy? What's this Buffy stuff?" Mrs. Freiburger asked.

"He's my toad," Owen said.

Richard groaned loudly.

"You are not to bring toads into the library. I'm sorry, Owen. Absolutely no animals."

"We're going to leave right away, anyway, Mrs. Freiburger. I found the books I was looking for," Richard said.

"Then I will check them out for you. Now. And please, boys, pick them up carefully." Mrs. Freiburger left Owen and Richard, just as Elke came forward to help them.

"Did we get kicked out?" she asked. "I didn't mean to let go, Owen. I just slipped."

"It's okay," Owen said, "but I could have lost Buffy."

"Hold on to him," Richard said. "Anyway we're going now."

Owen set Buffy in the bucket and tried to scrape up the dirt and pick up the pebbles that had bounced out. A smudge of mud stained the tan rug where Buffy's pond had spilled. Owen hoped that Mrs. Freiburger didn't see the mud. She would never let them back into the library again.

Owen waited in the wagon beneath the checkout counter. He watched Richard carry the stack of books carefully to the counter and pile them on it.

"I made a discovery, Owen. I'll show you when we get home."

Owen stretched up to look at the books, but Mrs. Freiburger had already flipped them over. Bleep, bleep went her scanner. Owen glanced at the fishbowl above him. Two bug-eyed fish swam around and around, swishing their fantails in the green weeds.

"Scoot over a little," Richard said, setting the books in the wagon.

Owen pulled Buffy closer to his chest. "I don't see why Buffy can't go in the library. Mrs. Freiburger lets fish come in. She has two of them up there."

Mrs. Freiburger heard Owen. "No toads, Owen. Not even in a bucket."

"Why?" Owen asked. Richard turned the wagon with a jerk and hurried toward the front door.

Before they got outside, Owen heard Mrs. Freiburger's answer. "Because my fish do not cause disturbances."

14
LIKE A TARGET

"Archery. Archery and You. Bow Hunters Guide." Owen read the titles of the books Richard had checked out. "Thanks a lot, Richard."

"No. Wait, Owen." Richard grabbed the thick blue book on the bottom. "Here."

"The Lives of Amphibians: Observations from the Field." Richard pointed to the title. "Do you know what amphibians are?"

"Of course," Owen said, insulted.

Richard opened the cover to show Owen a faded yellow sticker glued onto the inside cover. "From the library of Sinclair Snyder."

"It's Grandpa's book. Richard, this book belonged to Grandpa."

"He must have given it to the library."

"Grandma did. She told me. When he died." Owen added, "I wish we could have it."

"I'm not going to ask Mrs. Freiburger for it, are you?"

Owen shook his head. Mrs. Freiburger would never give them a library book to keep. They were lucky she even let them check out books.

Owen carried the book upstairs to the balcony porch. His leg still hurt, and he had to go up the stairs one at a time. Richard had put the key back in the door. Mom had never noticed it had been missing right after his accident. Owen didn't move the key to the outside. He didn't feel he had to. Richard wouldn't bother him. With Buffy beside him, he sat down and opened the book.

First, he just turned the pages and looked at all the pictures. Colored pictures, not photographs, and whoever drew them was really good. Not just toads, but frogs and lizards and red efts and salamanders, too. Owen especially liked their eyes.

"Toads' eyes are beautiful," he told Buffy. Then he found a whole chapter on North American toads and began to read.

By the time Richard yelled, "Mom's home. I'll go get my bow," Owen had found the part about how toads, all amphibians, can only live through the winter if they "seek refuge." Sometimes they go into a kind of sleep at the bottom of ponds that don't freeze or in caves or in the ground.

"Owen, hurry up!"

Owen finished the paragraph before he got up. He left the book on the porch. Limping, he took Buffy to his room, then went downstairs.

Richard was on the porch, waiting. "We'll go to the empty lot to shoot. Fred's going to meet us there."

Richard gave Owen a piggyback ride to the red wagon.

"Richard, what do you think would happen to a toad if it didn't hide someplace in the winter?"

"I don't know, Owen. I thought you were supposed to look these things up in your books." Richard began pulling the wagon up the alley.

"I did. I was just wondering. I mean, could a toad live all winter? You know, inside, where it's warm. Except there wouldn't be bugs to catch to feed it. The thing is, do toads really have to sleep in winter?"

"Look, Owen. Couldn't you just forget about toads for a minute and think about bows and arrows? I thought you wanted to come."

"I do." Owen decided not to say anything else about toads to Richard right now.

Fred was piling a bale of hay onto two bales that sat in front of the tumbledown shed. His bow was strung and lay on the ground near the plum tree. It was the same as two days ago. Richard and Fred and the bows and arrows. Except now Buffy wasn't in danger. Owen didn't have to charge into Richard and knock him down. Had he really knocked his brother down? Had he really been that mad? He looked at the empty lot. What a great place to be! No wonder Richard and Fred came here. The weeds were tall and wild-looking, and no one would come to bother them.

"Hey, Richard!" Fred looked up. "So Owen, how's the leg? How many stitches did you get?"

"I don't know. A bunch."

"Show me."

"I'd better not take the bandage off. It'll get germs in it or something." Owen didn't mention that he was afraid it would hurt to peel the tape off.

"I saw the stitches," Richard said. "There were lots."

That seemed to satisfy Fred. Owen felt relieved that no one was going to rip the bandage off.

Richard held up his long green fiberglass bow. He had already snapped the leather finger guard around his wrist and fastened a leather patch on the inside of his left arm between his elbow and wrist. "You have to wear these, Owen. Or the string will hurt your fingers. And you need the patch on your arm, too.

"Okay, Owen. Watch me." Richard stood tall, his left side toward the garage. He slipped an arrow onto the arrow guide of the bow, fitting the bowstring between the notches. Owen could see him take a deep breath, raise the bow, and pull back on the arrow. Thump, thwack! The arrow sailed into the target strung around the hay bales. The arrow wasn't smack in the bull's-eye, but it was close.

"You go so fast," Owen said. He would never be able to pull that bow back and let the arrow go the way Richard did.

Richard had five more arrows to shoot, and Fred had four in all. They took turns.

Swish. Thunk. Swish. Thunk.

Owen watched the bows rise and the arrows fly. He tried to guess where the arrows would hit.

"Yeah!" he shouted when Richard hit the bull's-eye.

Richard made it look so easy.

"When is it my turn?" Owen asked. "I want to shoot, too. You said you would show me how."

"Just one more round, Owen."

Finally all the arrows were stuck in the hay bale, and Fred went to pull them out. Richard showed Owen how to hold his bow.

"Do you want to stay in the wagon?"

"I don't know," Owen said. "Can people shoot in a wagon?"

"Why not? Don't you remember those Special Olympics Uncle Homer took us to? Guys in wheelchairs were shooting bows, and they were good."

"I remember," Owen said. "But they were older

than me, and I bet they practiced for years." He held the bow up and stared at the target, but it didn't feel right. "I guess I'll stand up."

Richard helped him out of the wagon.

Richard took an arrow from Fred and nocked it onto the bowstring. "You always put the arrow here, the nock point."

Owen noticed two strands of red string wound around the bowstring. Between the strands the bowstring was bare. Richard showed Owen how to hold the arrow between his fingers.

"Now look at the target. When you pull your arm back, keep your left elbow out a little. If you lock your elbow, the bowstring will clobber you on the arm."

Fred held up his left arm to show Owen an oval purple bruise. "It'll be black and blue and real sore."

Owen's left arm shook as he tried to hold the bow up and then pull back on the string with his right hand.

"Easy, Owen. You don't have to bend the bow in half."

"I can't." But Owen wanted to pull it back as far as Richard had and shoot just like his brother. He wanted to hit a bull's-eye the first time and hear Richard and Fred shout, "Way to go!" in amazement.

"Okay. Now just relax your fingers, and the arrow will fly."

Owen let go, and the arrow climbed up into the

air before it curved downward and dropped in front of the hay bales. Owen groaned.

"That's okay, Owen."

Owen was afraid Richard would take the bow away now because he was such a miserable shot. But Richard didn't. He let Owen shoot again. He helped him each time, again and again and again, until Owen hit the target.

"Not bad. If you keep practicing, you'll get a bull's-eye," Richard said. "You'll see. You can get as good as Fred and me."

A warm feeling rushed through Owen's body. "Do you think so?" Then he thought, If I get good, they'll let me shoot with them all the time.

"Sure," Richard said. "If you're good enough, we'll take you hunting. In the fall we're going to hunt deer. Aren't we, Fred? I haven't asked Dad yet, but I know he'll take us. He always takes me hunting in the fall."

"Do you really think I could go, too?" Owen had never been hunting, just target shooting that one time. Dad and Richard hunted a lot with guns, not bows. Sometimes they brought home a quail or rabbit. Owen didn't like to think about that. But most of the time they didn't bring anything home. They talked about hunting and looked at each other in a way that made Owen feel he had missed something.

Owen wondered if he would change his mind

about animals. He didn't want to hunt them or shoot them. Would he be like Richard and Dad when he got older? Maybe that happens when you grow up. Maybe he was growing up, because today, this afternoon, he had a powerful urge to go hunting with Richard and Dad and Fred. And he knew he could make it happen. All he had to do was learn how to shoot the bow. He concentrated on slipping the arrow into the nock point.

"Richard. Look!" Fred nudged Richard and pointed at a big gray pigeon waddling on the edge of the empty lot.

"Wow! He's big," Richard said. "I bet he came from the church up at the corner."

"Let's see who can hit him." Fred put an arrow in his bow. "We'll have to shoot at the same time. Before he flies away. Get your bow, Richard."

"No. Owen can try."

Owen looked at the pigeon. A chill replaced the warm glow he had just felt. Shoot a pigeon? With a bow and arrow?

"It's just like a target, Owen. Go ahead."

The bow suddenly felt too heavy to hold. Owen tried not to let his arm shiver or his hands shake.

"Hurry up, Owen," Fred urged. "Before he flies off."

Owen took a deep shaky breath and held the bow up. Just like a target, he told himself. Not a real pigeon, a target. He could hit that target. He could show Richard and Fred how good he was.

The gray bird cooed and warbled as it wobbled around pecking the ground. Then it stopped still and held up its head, as if listening. Owen could see its little brown eyes rimmed with black. It was looking at him. Maybe it knew that Owen was getting ready to send an arrow right into its puffy feathered chest.

"Now!" cried Fred.

Owen let the arrow loose and watched it slide along the yard where the pigeon had stood an instant before but was now flapping up into the air. Both arrows had missed. Owen dropped the bow with relief.

"Not bad."

Owen could hear regret in Richard's voice. If Richard had shot the bow, he wouldn't have missed.

"But be careful with my bow, will you?" Richard said.

"Owen, I can't believe your arrow came closer. You almost got that pigeon."

"Oh no," Owen said. "I missed by a mile." He wasn't disappointed. He felt like laughing or jumping up in the air. He wanted to celebrate because that gray pigeon had flown away from them, safe and alive and free. He wouldn't tell Richard and Fred how he felt. He wouldn't tell them how just then he had decided he was not going to be a great bow hunter after all.

15

SAVING BUFFY

The day Owen got his stitches out, he came home from the clinic, got on his bike, and rode around the block to see how it felt. His leg was a little stiff and sore, but he could ride fine. He slipped Buffy's bucket over the handlebars and rode to Grandma's.

She was weeding the garden in the backyard.

"I can help you, Grandma," Owen said.

"Owen, hi there. What a good idea! My old back has just about had it."

Owen set Buffy in the shade of the corner of the house. Then he showed Grandma his leg. "The stitches are all out now."

"Hmm." Grandma examined his cut. "Just a bit of a scar. How does it feel?"

"Fine. Dr. Fulham told me the scar would be all jagged if I hadn't had stitches."

"I'm happy to see you're all right now. I guess

you're not going to get in a fight again with rusted metal."

"Oh, Grandma." Owen laughed. He thought Grandma was joking. "I didn't," he said.

But when he looked up at her, she seemed serious. "I know," she said.

Maybe she did know what had happened, Owen thought. But how? Sometimes grown-ups knew things you never thought they would.

"I can't tell what really happened," he said. "I promised."

"You don't have to tell, Owen. I don't need to know any details."

A warm feeling of relief spread through Owen. Even if Grandma didn't know exactly what had happened, she knew, and Owen felt better knowing she knew.

Owen set to work pulling crabgrass from the bare ground between the radishes and thinning the lettuce plants. He tossed the weeds in piles and scooped them up to dump into the compost pile. When he was finished, Grandma gave him a glass of icy lemonade, and they sat on the back steps.

"Grandma, did you know Richard checked a book out of the library, and it belonged to Grandpa?"

"What book was that?" Grandma asked.

"It's big and blue and has great pictures of toads. Mom had to return it yesterday, though."

Grandma nodded, smiling. "And what would Richard want with a book on toads?"

"Not just toads—reptiles and amphibians. He got it for me the day we all went to the library." Owen stopped to look at Grandma and see if maybe Mrs. Freiburger had told her about their visit. No, she didn't frown or act as if she knew what had happened.

"Richard checked out books on archery. He taught me how to shoot a bow. I thought I would like it. But then he and Fred wanted me to shoot a pigeon, so I tried. I couldn't tell them, but I didn't want to hit it. You know what I mean. And then I missed, and I felt good about that."

Grandma smiled. "There is nothing wrong about not wanting to kill a pigeon. Your grandpa never harmed the creatures he studied. He always took them back to where he found them after he finished drawing. Sometimes he just sat and drew them right where they lived."

"I'd rather do that than shoot them."

"I guess that's the way you are, Owen."

Owen got up and gave Grandma a big hug. She hugged him right back.

"Thanks, Grandma."

Owen walked his bike across the yard with Buffy in his bucket hooked over the handlebars. He walked slowly, thinking about what Grandma had said.

*   *   *

The next morning Owen sat on the back steps to wait for Mom to leave for work and for Richard and Elke to get busy.

"Hey, Owen! Want to come shooting with me?" Richard trotted down the steps. His bow hung over his shoulder, and he had attached a quiver of arrows to his belt.

"No. Not today."

"But you're not doing anything."

"I have to help Grandma weed her garden."

"Gosh, Owen. The weeds'll keep. Come on."

Owen shook his head. "Maybe another time."

Richard looked puzzled. "You should be so lucky," he mumbled as he turned and headed up the alley.

As soon as Richard was out of sight, Owen picked up Buffy's bucket and went to his bike.

"This may feel a little funny," he warned Buffy. "Don't be scared. I have to put this lid on so you won't bounce out. There's holes in the top. You can breathe."

Owen slid the wire bucket holder over his handlebars and straddled his bike. He pedaled down the sidewalk as slowly as he could without falling. He turned right at the corner, then left onto the neighbor's driveway. From there he was out in the street without bumping over a curb. Mom would be mad if she knew he was riding in the street all the way to the cemetery. She might have let him go with Richard or

Elke or the cousins. But he didn't want to go with them. He wanted to go alone.

The brick-paved street was bumpy. Finally he turned up Fifth Street and rode down the smooth blacktop of Cypress Hill Road. The bucket swung back and forth, so Owen slowed down. He felt as if he had been riding for hours when he finally turned down the cinder road at Cypress Hill Cemetery.

His bike slowed to a stop in the cinders. He slipped off, catching the bike handle. He removed the bucket, slipped it over his right hand, and set his bike against a tree. He looked down the cinder road to the Snyder plot and the familiar cedar tree.

Owen sat beneath the cedar tree and removed the lid from Buffy's bucket. "Do you remember this place, Buffy?"

Owen studied his toad. Buffy was bigger than when he had found him. He seemed rounder, bulgier. The little stump where his leg should have been hadn't changed. Owen wished that Buffy could grow a new leg, the way some lizards grew tails that had broken off.

Should he put him back exactly where he had found him? Would Buffy really recognize the place? Owen wanted to find a safe spot. But where could he find a really safe spot for a toad in the wild? Owen tried not to think about the dangers. Buffy was smart. And now Buffy would be free.

Owen scooped up Buffy. The toad's rough dry skin felt cool. Owen warmed him for a minute, then he edged over to Grandpa's gravestone.

"Here he is, Grandpa. I'm letting Buffy loose." Owen held Buffy up and kissed him on the nose. "I'll see you again, Buffy."

When Owen set Buffy down on the thick grass, the toad sat as still as a statue. Owen nudged him, and Buffy hop-crawled toward the tall clump of grass beyond the gravestone.

"I'll be back. Every day." Owen wished that he could turn into a toad, a big toad so that he could take care of Buffy. He sat by the gravestone, watching and thinking long after the tall grass had quit moving. Then Owen emptied the rocks and dirt from the bucket into the grass over the grave. Water from Buffy's pond had spilled, and the dirt plopped out in damp clods.

When Owen finally stood up and turned around, he was startled to see Richard astride his bike, in the cinder road, watching him.

"You shouldn't come here by yourself, Owen. You'll get in trouble, and so will I."

"I'm old enough," Owen said. "If I ask Mom, she'll let me come." He thought to himself, I'll come anyway.

"I saw you. Why did you let Buffy go?" Richard

asked as they walked their bikes up the cinder road. "I thought you liked that toad."

Owen didn't know how to explain.

"If I had something I liked that much, I'd never let it go," Richard said.

Owen knew Richard hadn't said that to tease him or to boss him. Richard was telling the truth. When Richard made up his mind to get something he wanted, he got it, and when he got it, he kept it. That's the way he was.

How could Owen explain what he felt to Richard? He was different. He would never be like Richard, not in a million years. Even if he could explain, Owen didn't think that he could make Richard understand. Even if they were brothers. Even if they could keep each other's secrets. Even if they stopped being mean to each other.

"Grandpa always let them go," Owen said. "Did you know that sometimes toads live to be fifty years old? And they don't go very far from their home. I'm going to see Buffy again."

"Suit yourself, Owen. But you sure are a funny kid." Richard mounted his bike and perched on his seat for a moment before taking off. "I went over to Grandma's to look for you, you little liar. She said for us to stop by. She has some news for you, something about the library wanting to give you a big blue book."

"Grandpa's book!" Owen jumped on his bike.

Richard grinned and pedaled out to the middle of the street. Owen whirled the pedals around as fast as he could. He flew down the street after Richard, who seemed to be coasting. He caught up with his brother, and suddenly with a huge burst of energy he surged ahead. This time Owen would get there first.